PUFFIN CANADA

DIFFERENT DRAGONS

JEAN LITTLE is the award-winning author of
forty-four books for children. Her picture
books include *Once upon a Golden Apple*
and *Revenge of the Small Small*. Her novel
Willow and Twig won the Mr. Christie Book
Award, *His Banner Over Me* won the 1996
Violet Downey Book Award, and *Gruntle
Piggle Takes Off* was nominated for a
Governor General's Award for illustration.
Her work has been translated into eighteen
languages. She lives in Guelph, Ontario.

Also by Jean Little

Different Dragons

JEAN LITTLE

PUFFIN
CANADA

PUFFIN CANADA

Published by the Penguin Group

Penguin Group (Canada), 90 Eglinton Avenue East, Suite 700, Toronto, Ontario, Canada M4P 2Y3
(a division of Pearson Canada Inc.)

Penguin Group (USA) Inc., 375 Hudson Street, New York, New York 10014, U.S.A.
Penguin Books Ltd, 80 Strand, London WC2R 0RL, England
Penguin Ireland, 25 St Stephen's Green, Dublin 2, Ireland (a division of Penguin Books Ltd)
Penguin Group (Australia), 250 Camberwell Road, Camberwell, Victoria 3124, Australia
(a division of Pearson Australia Group Pty Ltd)
Penguin Books India Pvt Ltd, 11 Community Centre, Panchsheel Park, New Delhi – 110 017, India
Penguin Group (NZ), 67 Apollo Drive, Rosedale, North Shore 0632, New Zealand
(a division of Pearson New Zealand Ltd)
Penguin Books (South Africa) (Pty) Ltd, 24 Sturdee Avenue, Rosebank, Johannesburg 2196, South Africa

Penguin Books Ltd, Registered Offices: 80 Strand, London WC2R 0RL, England

First published in Viking Kestrel by Penguin Group (Canada), a division of Pearson Canada Inc., 1986
Published in Puffin Canada paperback by Penguin Group (Canada), a division of Pearson Canada Inc., 1988
Published in this edition, 2005

6 7 8 9 10 (WEB)

Copyright © Jean Little, 1986

Manufactured in Canada.

LIBRARY AND ARCHIVES CANADA CATALOGUING IN PUBLICATION

Little, Jean, 1932–
Different dragons / Jean Little.

First published: Markham, Ont. : Viking Kestrel, 1986.
ISBN 0-14-331230-8

I. Title.

PS8523.I77D53 2005   jC813'.54   C2005-902720-7

Visit the Penguin Group (Canada) website at **www.penguin.ca**

Special and corporate bulk purchase rates available; please see
www.penguin.ca/corporatesales or call 1 800 810 3104, ext. 2477 or 2474

Contents

Not That Kind of Boy

"Wake up, Ben," Dad said. "We'll be there soon."

Ben Tucker was not really asleep. He heard what his father said. But he stayed slumped down as far as his seatbelt would let him. He kept his eyes shut. If he woke up, they would be almost at Aunt Rose's house. Maybe, if he kept very still and did not open his eyes, Dad would change his mind and take him back home.

"Benjamin Tucker," Ben's father said, "don't you want to see the house I lived in when I was your age?"

Ben did want to see it. He had heard so much about the big old stone house in Guelph, where his father and his uncle and aunt had lived when they were kids. He just did not want to have to stay in it, not without Mum and Dad and Jimmy. He didn't even know Aunt Rose. Oh, he had met her. She had come to visit them in Vancouver. But that had been ages ago, when he was little. He couldn't even remember what she looked like.

Maybe she hated kids. Jimmy said she did. He had laughed when he said it, but it might be true. Jimmy ought to know. He was six years older than Ben was, and a lot bigger. And Jimmy had visited Aunt Rose last summer, when she lived away up in Hearst.

Now Aunt Rose had moved back into the old family home which had been rented for years. She was having part of the upstairs turned into an apartment. She had asked Ben's family to come for a visit before the apartment was rented. Right now she had lots of spare rooms. Ben would have been happy to go with his family, but that was not what was going to happen. He was to go there first, on his own, and the rest were not coming until suppertime on Sunday.

It was Dad's idea. He said it was Ben's turn to go somewhere without the rest of them. He said Ben would enjoy it. Jimmy was going to stay with a friend he'd made at camp last summer. And Dad and Mum had signed up to go to some dumb weekend conference.

So Ben was to stay at Aunt Rose's by himself. He had told them he didn't want to go, but they didn't care. Dad just said it would be good for him. Ben had never guessed that Dad could be so mean. How could they make him stay with this stranger for a whole weekend! This was only Friday. How was he going to get through the hours and hours until the others came? He would be there without anyone he knew for two whole days and two whole nights!

"Hey," Dad tried again. "I asked you a question. Aren't you speaking to me?"

Still pretending not to hear, Ben squeezed his eyes more tightly shut. That made two big tears roll out and slide down his cheeks. He gave a sad little sniff, too. There. That would let Dad know how he was feeling.

"Oh, Ben, don't start that again," Mr. Tucker said. He sounded tired. "You're too big to be such a crybaby. You're going to have a wonderful time. Your Aunt Rose knows what boys like."

"She can't know," Ben muttered. "She hasn't any boys."

"So what? She does know. She writes books for boys, remember. Not every boy has a writer for an aunt. It will be exciting for you having this chance to get to know her. You ought to be proud. You are going to visit a real live author. Think of that!"

Big deal, Ben thought. Was there such a thing as an unreal live author? Would he still have to go if she were a real dead one? He almost grinned but stopped himself in time. He didn't want Dad to catch him smiling.

"Tell the truth," Dad coaxed. "Aren't you really looking forward to meeting her? You must at least be curious."

Ben was. He couldn't help it. He was proud, too. He had seen Aunt Rose's books in the bookstore and in the library at school. Mum had read some of them out loud to him. They were great books, filled with magical adventures. When his teacher, Miss Morris, had heard he was going to see his famous aunt as soon as school ended, she had asked Ben to get her autograph. Some of the other kids had been jealous.

"You are a lucky boy," Miss Morris had said, "having Rose Tucker for an aunt."

Ben had felt lucky then. But not now. He wished Dad would stop trying to talk him around. Even if every single thing he said was true, Ben was not going to feel happy about this visit.

"Her books are all about boys who run away from home to fight dragons and find treasure. I'm not that kind of boy. She won't like me," he burst out, his voice shaking.

Dad did not say anything for a long moment. When he did answer, his words startled Ben.

"Everybody has to fight a dragon sometime," he said slowly. "You have different dragons to fight, that's all. I think you might even slay one or two this weekend."

Ben stared at his father. Had he gone crazy? Was Aunt Rose a dragon? Was that what he meant? No. It must be some dumb grown-up joke.

"Rose is really glad you are coming," Dad said. "She told me so herself. She'll show you all around the old house. When we come, you'll be the expert. You'll get ahead of your big brother for once. Maybe you'll have so much fun that you won't want Sunday afternoon to come."

Ben jerked around and glared at his father. "I will not have a good time," he yelled. At a look from Dad, he stopped shouting, but he kept on talking fast. "Why can't I go with you and Mum? Jimmy says Aunt Rose is really mean."

Mr. Tucker sighed. He took a deep breath.

"If your brother did say that, you know he was only teasing. You also know why you can't come with us. We've told you often enough. We are going to a conference. No children will be there. Your mother and I have not been away for a whole weekend by ourselves since you were a baby. If we don't go soon, we'll be too old to travel."

Ben knew that his father was kidding. He and Mum were old but not that old. Dad was trying to make him smile. But Ben didn't feel like smiling. He turned his head away and looked out the window.

Dad pulled off to the side of the road. He stopped the car and shifted so that he could look at Ben. Gently he drew Ben around so that they faced each other. When he spoke, his voice was deep and serious.

"Ben, you're old enough now to start thinking of

somebody besides yourself," he said. "Don't you think Mum deserves a holiday?"

Ben squirmed. That was a trick question. If he said she did, Dad would think that everything was all right. It wasn't. Why couldn't Mum think about him instead? He knew better than to say that out loud. So he just sat there and said nothing at all. That was the only safe thing to do.

Dad spoke sharply for the first time.

"Whether you like it or not, you are going to stay at Rose's for a couple of days," he snapped. "If you have made up your mind to be miserable, you probably will be. If you make the best of it instead, you'll enjoy yourself. That's up to you. But stop sulking. Grow up, Ben."

Ben's chin came up with a jerk. He bit his lip to keep it from trembling. But he couldn't make any words come out because of the big lump in his throat.

Maybe Dad guessed. He gave Ben's knee a comforting squeeze and spoke more gently. "I want you to try an experiment, Benjamin Tucker. Do you think you could at least try to have a good time at Rose's? I think you might surprise yourself if you'll only try."

Ben knew it wouldn't work. He was going to have a terrible time. He thought of what his brother Jimmy had really said. "She won't let you keep the hall light on like a baby," he had jeered.

Had Jimmy only been teasing? Ben could not always tell

when he was fooling and when he wasn't.

Dad reached into his pocket. He pulled out one of his big handkerchiefs and handed it to Ben. Ben wiped his eyes.

"How about it?" Mr. Tucker asked. "Will you give it a try?"

"Okay. I'll try," Ben said in a small, husky voice. Dad gave him a big smile. It changed his face so much that Ben blinked. Had his father really been worried about him? It looked like it.

"Good for you, Ben." His father started the car up again. "I was talking to Rose on the phone last night," he said as he drove. "I wasn't going to say anything, but it might help. She told me she has a big surprise for you, something you will really like, I'll bet. She didn't say what it was, but it must be something pretty special."

Ben felt better. A surprise for him! Did that mean a present?

Suddenly the car turned into a driveway.

"Here we are," Dad said. "And there's Rose in the garden."

Ben gulped. He grabbed his father's arm and held on tight.

"Promise you'll come as soon as you can on Sunday. And that you won't not come, no matter what," he begged.

"We'll be here in time for supper if we have to hire a plane," his father promised.

2

Aunt Rose

Ben got out of the car slowly. His stomach felt as
though it was doing flip-flops. He was scared to
look at Aunt Rose. He knew without turning to
look that his aunt was coming across the grass to meet them.
Dad hurried toward her without waiting for Ben.

"Hello, stranger," Aunt Rose said.

She didn't really mean Dad was a stranger. You wouldn't
hug a stranger the way she was hugging his father.

"Stranger yourself," Dad said, laughing and hugging her
back. "I'd have known you anywhere, fat as you are."

That made Ben stop looking at the ground. He stared at
his aunt, instead. He remembered her right away. She was

not a total stranger, after all. She was not fat, either. Dad must be kidding. She was tall, almost as tall as Ben's father. She had short fair hair, only a little darker than Ben's. And her eyes were smiling at him over Dad's shoulder.

As his father let go of her and turned to draw him forward, Ben stood as tall as he could. He did not smile. He even frowned a little. He had a feeling that if he smiled back at this aunt of his, she might kiss him. Ben did not want to be kissed, not by somebody he didn't know, even if he did remember her face now.

Maybe she guessed how he felt. She came toward him, still smiling, and just stood and looked at him for a moment. Then she spoke.

"Hi, Tommy," she said.

Ben scowled. He hated being called Tommy. Grown-ups thought it was cute because of that dumb poem about Little Tommy Tucker. Ben and Jimmy agreed that the poem was soppy and being called Tommy Tucker made them both feel like dopes. No wonder Jimmy hadn't liked Aunt Rose if she was that kind of grown up!

Then Aunt Rose burst out laughing.

"I'm sorry, Ben," she said. "I just wanted to see if you would make the same disgusted face your father always made when people called him Tommy. You do, exactly the same. You look so much like him when he was your age, too. I promise never to call you that again."

Ben couldn't help smiling back then. He liked it when people said he looked like Dad. And she did sound sorry. Maybe Jimmy had only been teasing when he had said she was mean.

He couldn't think of what to say. Perhaps she guessed that. She turned back to talk with his father as they started up the front steps of the big old house.

The house seemed strange to Ben. For one thing, it was made of stone. In Vancouver there weren't any stone houses. It was a tall house, too. Ben's home was all on one floor, but this house had three big windows upstairs. There were two more wide windows, one on each side of the front door. The door was double, like the windows, with a brass knocker on each side. It was all so big that Ben could hardly believe his eyes.

Was there an attic? He craned his neck looking for any sign of one. He had never been in a house with an attic, but this one was so huge that it ought to have one. In Aunt Rose's first book, a boy found a secret treasure hidden in an attic. Ben couldn't see any tiny cobwebby windows up under the eaves, but maybe they were on the other side of the house.

"Come on, Ben, stop dreaming," Dad said. "We're waiting for you."

Ben jumped. He felt his face getting red. He ran up the steps and in through the big front door Dad was holding open for him.

He stared around the shadowy front hall. It was spooky. Then he saw the banister Dad had told them about. You could slide down it or you could straddle the flat round part at the bottom and pretend you were riding a horse. Neat!

"Have you time for a cup of coffee before you go, John?" Aunt Rose was asking.

Ben's stomach tightened. Dad glanced at his watch.

"I really should be leaving," he began.

Then he looked down at Ben's hand, clutching his sleeve.

"I guess I can spare ten minutes. If you show us where you're putting Ben, I can help get him settled."

"I've put Ben in my old room," Aunt Rose said. "Let's go up the back stairs."

Ben followed her. He carried the small suitcase with his clothes inside. He thought he looked grown-up, but he was glad Dad was right behind him.

The back stairs opened out of the kitchen. They were steep and narrow and a bit dark. Ben had never been in a house with two sets of stairs before. These stairs had walls on both sides instead of a banister. If he lived here, Ben thought he would use the front stairs.

"This way," his aunt said, opening a door. "You get to choose, Ben, whether you want to sleep up or down."

Ben stared at the bunks. He had never slept in a bunk bed. The top one had a neat ladder going up to it, but it looked very high in the air. Ben liked the bottom bunk better. It would be like having his own little cave. Would they think he was a sissy if he took the bottom one? He searched Dad's face.

"Well, which will it be?" his father asked, smiling. He was leaving it up to Ben. And Jimmy wasn't here to make fun of him.

"I'd rather sleep in the bottom one," he said in a low voice.

"Fine," Aunt Rose said. "Jimmy chose the bottom bunk when he stayed with me last summer. He said he was scared he'd roll out of the top one, although nobody has fallen out of it yet. There's a light right here at the head, which you can turn on when you want to read. I think that's what Jimmy really liked."

Ben gazed at the bed light. If he got scared in the dark, all he had to do was reach up and turn it on. And Jimmy had been scared. Jimmy!

"It's great," he breathed.

He put his bag down on top of the bed. He undid it. Then, as he opened it, he saw his pajamas right on top. He swallowed.

"How about that cup of coffee, Rose?" Dad said all at once. "Ben can explore up here later."

"You'll have to settle for instant coffee if you're in such a rush."

"Instant will be fine," Ben's father said, following her out of the room and down the stairs.

Ben ran after him and caught hold of his hand.

"Don't tell Mum I'm going to sleep in a bunk bed," he said. "Let me show her on Sunday."

Dad grinned down at him.

"I won't say a word about it," he promised. "You'll have a lot to tell us when we get here."

He drank his coffee standing up.

"I really do have to go now," he said, heading for the front door. "We have to be at the conference by eight o'clock. You behave, Ben. See that he does, Rose. It's good of you to have him on his own like this."

"I'm glad to have him to myself," Aunt Rose said, putting one hand lightly on Ben's shoulder. "We'll get to know each other better without the rest of you getting in our way. Have a wonderful time, John. Drive carefully."

Dad gave them both a quick hug. Ben felt tears coming into his eyes. If Dad didn't go fast, he knew he was going to cry.

Dad must have known. He ran down the front steps, jumped into the car, waved once and was gone.

Ben wanted to run after the car and shout at his father to come back. But then he heard Aunt Rose's voice.

"Ben Tucker," she said, "what do you like best of all to eat?"

He turned slowly and looked at her. He was so surprised that he stopped wanting to cry. "If it isn't too, too complicated, you and I could make it for supper," she said.

"Just don't say Baked Alaska or chocolate eclairs. I tried those once and they tasted terrible."

Ben did like chocolate eclairs, but they weren't his favourite thing. He had never heard of Baked Alaska.

"I like spaghetti best," he said at last. His voice shook a little and he had to rub away some tears with the back of his hand. His aunt did not seem to notice.

"What a relief!" she cried. "I'm a great cook when it comes to spaghetti. You'll have to help, though, and make sure I do it just the way you like it. I have a pumpkin pie for dessert. Do you like pumpkin pie?"

Ben grinned. "Is there whipped cream?"

"There will be when you whip it," his aunt said.

A bunk bed. A light he could turn on whenever he wanted. Spaghetti, just the way he liked it. Pumpkin pie with whipped cream for supper and the surprise yet to come! Thinking of all these things, Ben felt much better. Aunt Rose was nice, too, not a bit like a dragon.

"I like lots of sauce and lots of cheese," he told her, "and I like little meatballs, with no onions in them."

His aunt leaned down all at once and kissed him on top of his head.

"No onions, on my word of honour," she said.

Being kissed wasn't all that bad.

3.

The Surprise

"I have a surprise for you," Aunt Rose said. "I hope you'll like it. But we'd better get started on our cooking or we won't be ready when it arrives."

"What is the surprise?" Ben asked, trotting after her as she led the way to the kitchen.

"If I told you that, it wouldn't be a surprise, would it?"

"I guess not," Ben had to admit. "When will it … be here?"

"About seven-thirty," his aunt said. "Do you think you can wait till then?"

Ben nodded politely, but it did seem a long time to wait. It was just five o'clock now.

"I'll keep you busy. Then the time will go faster. You can start by whipping the cream for the pie."

Ben had never whipped cream before. At home he and Jimmy helped with the dishes, but they hardly ever got to cook. Whipping cream wasn't hard to do, though. He had watched his mother do it millions of times. It was simple.

"Do you know how?" Aunt Rose asked as she got out a bowl, the carton of whipping cream, some sugar and the bottle of vanilla.

"Sure," Ben said. He did know how. He was sure he did. You beat the cream first. Then you put in the sugar and vanilla at the end. It was a cinch.

Aunt Rose was busy filling a big pot with water. That would be for the spaghetti. She wasn't even watching him. He dumped the cream into the bowl, stuck the beaters in, turned them on and began to whip.

He felt great, standing there, in charge of the whirring electric mixer. He flicked the switch from Medium to High and back again. He beat and beat the cream. All at once, it began to get thicker.

Ben turned the beaters off and looked at it. It seemed about right. He'd better be sure to beat it enough, though. He turned the beaters on again.

"That must be about done," Aunt Rose said over her shoulder.

"Just about," Ben said. He kept on beating. Then he

turned the beaters off and looked at the cream again.

It was full of queer little yellowish flecks.

Ben stared down at it. Should he tell Aunt Rose? He didn't want to. Maybe once he beat in the sugar and vanilla, it would be all right. That was probably what it needed.

Ben measured out a couple of spoonfuls of sugar. He dumped them in. Then, with the greatest care, he added the vanilla. Feeling nervous, he switched the beaters on once more.

Aunt Rose turned to look at him.

"Be careful, Ben, or you'll whip it to butter," she warned.

Ben's heart sank. He peered into the bowl, hoping against hope that the bits of yellow would have disappeared. They were bigger. He *had* whipped the cream to butter. He stood very still, his head hanging. How was he going to tell his aunt?

"Benjamin Tucker, don't look like that," Aunt Rose said. "The sky hasn't fallen. What's wrong? *Did* you whip it to butter?"

She sounded as though she were laughing. Ben felt awful. His aunt came and stood beside him. She looked down at what he had done.

"I've always wondered how pumpkin pie would taste with butter on it," she said. She was really laughing now.

"I'm sorry," Ben said miserably. "I thought I knew how." His voice trailed off. The ache was back in his throat.

He looked up. Aunt Rose's eyes were twinkling down at him. He gazed at the blobs of butter and did his best to smile.

"Don't worry, Ben," Aunt Rose said, putting the bowl in the fridge. "I've done the same thing myself. I think we'll make this into sweet butter and eat it with muffins some other time. I have some more whipping cream I was going to use tomorrow. If at first you don't succeed …"

This time, Ben stopped whipping at exactly the right moment. Supper was delicious. He had two helpings of spaghetti. He wanted to have more pie, too, but he didn't have any room left.

While they did the dishes, Aunt Rose told him funny stories about when she and Dad were kids.

"What is your bedtime?" she asked when they had finished.

"Nine o'clock on weekends," Ben told her.

The thought of going to bed here, even in the neat bunk bed with his own light, made Ben feel lonesome again.

"How about a game of Snakes and Ladders?" Aunt Rose said quickly. Ben didn't think much of Snakes and Ladders. He wondered if she had Monopoly. Before he could make up his mind whether it would be rude to ask, the doorbell chimed.

"The surprise has arrived!" Aunt Rose said, going to answer the door. Ben was right on her heels. But when they got to the front hall, he heard something outside the door making a lot of noise. Whatever the surprise was, it banged and thumped and scratched.

Ben felt uneasy, all at once. He drew back.

Then Aunt Rose pulled open the door. In shot a very tall man gripping a leash. At the end of the leash was an enormous, cream coloured dog with floppy golden ears. The dog made straight for Ben. He was a Labrador retriever. To Ben he looked as big as a lion.

Ben screamed and ducked behind Aunt Rose. He hated dogs even more than he hated the dark. Dogs were dangerous. They jumped at you and knocked you down and bit you. Sometimes they even killed people. One of the kids had brought a story to school about somebody being attacked by a savage dog and nearly dying. Miss Morris had said they shouldn't trust strange dogs. When a large stray had got into the school one day, she had kept the door of their classroom shut until she was sure it was gone. She wouldn't even let anybody go to the bathroom.

"It might be vicious," she had said.

Mum and Dad said it was foolish to be so afraid of dogs. But Miss Morris had been scared. And she was a teacher!

"He won't hurt you," the man half shouted over the racket the huge dog's paws were making. "Labs are friendly. He's young and foolish but he's harmless, honest. He gets very excited still when he goes visiting and he likes boys. He just wants to play. Stop it, Gully, you idiot! His name is Gully. It's short for Gulliver Gallivant."

Ben did not care what the monster's name was. He had both arms wound tightly around Aunt Rose from behind. He wished she were a tree so he could climb up her. He was shaking so hard his teeth chattered.

Aunt Rose reached around and tried to pull him loose. He hid his face against her back and hung on for dear life.

"You'd better shut Gully in the kitchen for now, Bob," she said at last. "I should have told Ben what was coming and let him get used to the idea first. John said that he was frightened of dogs, but I didn't take it seriously. Gully is such a lamb. But maybe he does take getting used to."

The man looked worried. Gully was pulling hard on the leash. His tail was thwacking against the man's leg. It sounded like a whip to Ben.

"I'm sorry I didn't know sooner," Bob said. "I could have made other plans for Gully."

"Don't be silly," Aunt Rose told him. "Put Gully in the kitchen now and run along. As soon as Ben sees how gentle the dog is, they'll make friends in no time."

Make friends with a dog? Never!

Ben could hear Bob dragging Gully across the room. Gully did not want to go out to the kitchen. Bob had to pull hard. Once he got him there, he spoke in a loud, firm voice.

"Gulliver, stay!"

Then he shut the kitchen door.

Ben held his breath and listened. Would Gully charge right through the closed door? He didn't. He whimpered. Then Ben could hear him running around, exploring the kitchen.

Bob came back. Ben had loosened his grip on his aunt and was now peering around her. The tall man gave him a troubled smile.

"Hi, Ben," he said. "I'm Bob Wells. My wife and I live just up the block. I'm sorry our surprise has been such a flop. But you'll like Gully when you get to know him. You'll have to help Rose look after him. He's staying for the weekend, too. Rose, I left the bag with his stuff on top of your fridge."

Aunt Rose pulled Ben in front of her. Now, keeping one arm around him, she sank down on the nearest chair.

"Ben, don't be so silly," she said. "Gully hasn't a mean bone in his body. Did you see how beautiful he is?"

Ben shook his head. He would not meet her eyes. He did not think Gulliver was beautiful. He thought he was horrible. Maybe *he* was the dragon Dad had talked about. If he was, he'd be the one to slay Ben, if he got the chance. That dog probably ate a couple of boys every day for breakfast.

"Well, I've got to get going," Bob said, when Ben made no answer. "Goodbye, Rose, and good luck."

Once the front door shut behind him, Aunt Rose and Ben stared at each other. Then Aunt Rose began to laugh again. That made Ben mad. This wasn't like whipping the cream to butter. This was serious. Ben wanted to go home right away.

"Can he stay in the kitchen till Sunday?" he asked.

"He can stay there till you're in bed, anyway," his aunt said. "Tomorrow will be soon enough for you to make friends."

Ben did not argue. If he started talking about how he felt, he'd cry. And he was not going to cry in front of this aunt who kept laughing over nothing.

"Can I go to bed now?" he said.

Aunt Rose glanced at her watch.

"It's only eight o'clock," she told him. "You said your bedtime wasn't till nine. Wouldn't you like to play a game? Or I could read to you, if you'd rather."

Ben looked down at his feet. She'd want to read a story about a brave boy who loved dogs more than anything.

"I guess I'm tired," he muttered, feeling his face get hot. "I just want to go to bed."

Aunt Rose looked sorry about everything, but she just said, "If that's what you want, then bed it shall be. Do you need any help? Would you like to have a bath?"

"No," Ben said. "I had a bath this morning."

"Go ahead, then. I'll come up later to look in on you."

Ben climbed the stairs with his back very straight. He turned on the light at the head of his bunk. He opened his bag and reached for his pajamas. There was something hard wrapped up in the bottoms. He undid it. It was a pocket-sized flashlight! Mum must have put it in so he wouldn't be scared at night. He swallowed, but the lump in his throat just got bigger.

He left the flashlight in the suitcase and put his pajamas on. Even though he had a light to read with, he didn't get out the book he had brought. He felt too miserable to read. He didn't even brush his teeth. He got under the covers and pulled them up to his chin. His hands were shaking. He reached up and switched off his light.

Nothing, not the bunk or the light or the supper, was nice anymore. He did not want to stay here. He wanted to go home. He wanted Mum and Dad. He even wanted Jimmy. Sunday afternoon seemed a hundred years away.

4

The Mysterious Noises

Whack-whack-whack. *Flip-flap. Thump-whack.*

Ben Tucker opened his eyes. He stared up at the bunk above him. For a moment he could not figure out what it was. The light was coming from the wrong place, too. At home his bedroom window was right across from his bed. In this room he could tell it was in the wall at the foot of the bunk.

Bunk! He remembered in a flash. He was at Aunt Rose's house, and the first night of the weekend was over. Tomorrow his family would come. Ben smiled.

Flippity-flip. Whack-whack-whack!

Ben turned his head so that he could see what was making the strange noises. Then he froze.

Right next to his bed stood an enormous dog. A gigantic dog, a positive monster of a dog. Gully!

Ben gasped. He almost screamed, but he caught his breath in time. He must not let Gully know how scared he was. Dogs could smell your fear. "They only attack people who are afraid of them," Jimmy had told him once. Ben stopped breathing. Maybe, if he did not move a muscle, Gully would go away.

Gully stayed right where he was. He was standing so close that Ben could have reached out and patted him. He had his mouth open so that he looked as if he were laughing. Ben did not think it was a friendly laugh. All he saw were Gully's big, sharp teeth. As Ben stared at him, Gully began to wag his tail. It thwacked against the bedside table.

Whack-whack-whack.

Then, as Ben still lay stiffly, holding his breath and praying Aunt Rose would come, the big dog shook himself. His ears flapped and his skin moved, somehow, as though it was too big for him, and his feet jigged a bit.

Flip-flap, thump, whackity-thump.

It was Gully who had made all the mysterious noises. Ben felt as though he was going to burst. He had to begin breathing again. He took the smallest breaths he could. He wanted to call Aunt Rose for help, but he was afraid to make a sound. He remembered a show he had seen on TV, where a policeman with a dog just Gully's size had cornered a bad guy.

"Make one false move," the policeman had said, "and Thor will tear you apart."

The man had reached for his gun anyway. Moving like a streak of lightning, the dog had flown at him and knocked him to the ground.

Ben shivered. He could still hear the man's scream.

Gully kept wagging his tail. That was a good sign. Had that police dog wagged his tail before he sprang? Ben couldn't remember.

Please, God, make him go away, he prayed silently.

Gully did not go. Instead he came even closer. Ben clutched at his sheet and opened his mouth to shriek. Before he could do it, though, a huge tongue had sloshed across his clenched hand. Ben was so astonished at the feel of it that he did not even squeak. Gulliver Gallivant's tongue was very soft, very wet and as big as a bath towel. It washed the back of Ben's hand thoroughly and then went on to lick his wrist and bare arm.

Maybe he's checking to see how I taste, Ben thought. Maybe any second now he'll take a big bite.

But he didn't believe it, not really. The big tongue was too gentle. It sort of tickled. Gully did not seem to notice his fear.

"Good boy," Ben said in a cracked whisper. "Good boy."

Gully's tail went twice as fast. It beat the bedside table as if it were a drum.

"Gully, where are you? Come and get it," Aunt Rose called from downstairs.

The large cream-coloured dog with the golden ears whirled around so fast that his paws skidded on the bare floor. He bounded out of the room without looking back once. Ben listened to him charging down the stairs. He did not slow down. He went full speed all the way to the bottom. He sounded like a whole stampede of dogs.

Very carefully, Ben slid out of bed. He tiptoed to the door and shut it tight. Then he went back to the bunk, sank down on it and shook.

"I hate dogs," he muttered. "I don't care if they're friendly or not. I don't like them and nobody can make me."

The back of his hand was still wet from Gully's tongue. Ben scrubbed it dry on the sheet. He'd have to use soap later to get the dog germs off.

He didn't know what he ought to do next. He wanted to crawl back into bed and go to sleep until his family came, but he knew Aunt Rose wouldn't let him. Besides, he was hungry.

He got up. He would get dressed right away while it was safe. He put on his clothes in such a hurry that he got his T-shirt on back to front and had to take it off and put it on again frontwards. He was glad nobody was there to see.

He was really hungry now. But where was that awful dog? Ben went to the door and laid his ear against it. As he stood there, somebody knocked on the other side of the door. Ben jumped.

"Benjamin Tucker, are you up?" Aunt Rose's voice asked.

Ben opened the door. His aunt smiled down at him.

"Don't worry," she said, as if she knew all about the cold, scared feeling in the pit of his stomach. "Gully is outside. One of the neighbour children is playing with him. How did you like sleeping in my old room?"

"It was fine," Ben said politely.

"Would you like to take a look at your father's old room before breakfast?"

Ben nodded. He pushed his worry about Gully to the back of his mind. He really did want to see the room his father had slept in when he was a kid.

He followed Aunt Rose across the landing, up three steps and through a door to a wide hall with a tall double window at the far end. Ben realized that the tall window must be one of the big ones at the front of the house. He had never been in such a big house before. He stared at five more doors. The two open ones led to a bathroom and a little kitchen.

"How many rooms are there in this place?" he asked.

Dad had read *The Secret Garden* to him once. Misslethwaite Manor, in the book, had had over one hundred rooms. Their house in Vancouver had seven, eight if you counted the TV room in the basement.

Aunt Rose paused to think.

"Five bedrooms upstairs," she said. "Two small ones off the back hall and three larger ones in here. A small junk room that I've had converted into a kitchen. Two bathrooms, one front and one back. And downstairs there's my study, my kitchen, the dining room and the living room. Then there's a small bathroom down there plus my bedroom. How many is that?"

Ben wasn't sure, but he thought it had been fourteen. Wow! No wonder Dad liked this house so much. She hadn't counted the halls, either. The front hall was bigger than their living room in Vancouver.

Aunt Rose laughed at his look of astonishment.

"I know," she said. "It is far too big a place for one person to live in. But I've always loved large houses. And I'm going to rent this front part, don't forget. I've fixed up these two rooms on the left for your parents and Jimmy. Your father's old room was this front one."

Ben hurried to peer in. It was a big room with one of the wide double windows looking out onto the street. But it was disappointing. It was just like his parents' bedroom at home, not like a kid's room at all. Ben turned away.

"Here's where I'm putting Jimmy," Aunt Rose said.

Ben looked. It was an even larger room, newly painted and very empty except for one bed and a straight chair. "It's nice," Ben murmured. He wished there would be something interesting, something different. Misslethwaite Manor had been filled with neat old stuff.

They returned to the hall. There was one more closed door.

"Who slept in that one?" Ben asked, pointing.

"Our grandmother," Aunt Rose said. "I haven't finished painting it yet. Once your dad arrives, he can give me a hand. The ceilings are so high. Do you want to see it, too?"

Ben did. She went ahead of him again, talking as she went.

"Grandma was very strict about us never setting foot inside her door unless she had her eye on us. I still feel a bit strange coming in here without her permission, even though she died twenty years ago. Watch out for the ladder, Ben."

Ben dodged the stepladder which stood just inside the door. He stared around the empty room, trying to imagine Dad wanting to come into it when he was a kid. He couldn't. It didn't look one bit mysterious or interesting, just very bare.

"I'd better open the window and let some fresh air in here," Aunt Rose muttered. "I don't want your parents not to be able to sleep because of paint fumes."

While she was busy doing this, Ben went over to the closet and looked inside. It was just a very large closet, the kind you could walk into, with shelves going up one side and a rod for hanging up your clothes on the other. Then he glanced up.

Above his head, away up in the roof of the closet, there was a trap door!

Ben stood still and stared. He had always wanted to explore a house with trap doors and secret passages and locked rooms. No house he'd ever been inside had anything exciting like that. And now here, in his very own aunt's house, there was an actual trap door leading who knew where. He turned quickly to ask her about it.

Bang! Bang!

Aunt Rose was whamming the sash of the window to get it loose. Then she had to heave hard to raise it. By the time she had dusted her hands off on her jeans and turned to face him, he had changed his mind about asking.

The closet was still unpainted. Maybe nobody had noticed the trap door yet. Maybe, if Dad and Aunt Rose hadn't been allowed in there, he was the only one who knew about it. No. Somebody had been in there after his great-grandmother had died because her things were gone. But whoever had cleared out the closet might never have looked up.

There was, at least, a chance that the trap door was his secret. This wasn't very likely, he knew, but it was possible. And if he was the only one who'd spotted it, as soon as he got time to himself, he'd find some way to get up there.

Ben shivered just thinking about it. But he was more excited than scared.

It might be dark up there, but he didn't mind the dark in the daytime. At least, he didn't think he did. And maybe it wasn't dark.

Maybe it led to an attic full of hidden treasures.

Some Strange Girl

"Y ou must be hungry, Ben," Aunt Rose said. "Let's get you some breakfast. We can go down the front way. I want to leave the front door open to help air the house. Go ahead and slide down the banister. Your father always did."

Ben swooped to the bottom while she was still just halfway down. It was great. He slithered off and followed her to the kitchen.

"This is your place," Aunt Rose said.

Ben slid into his chair and stared down at the writing on his placemat. The letters spelled BEN'S PLACE.

"Hey, it has my name on it," he said.

"So it does," Aunt Rose said. "I saw it in a store downtown one day. I thought it would make you feel at home."

She was nice. Jimmy was crazy. Ben smiled at her. Then he remembered how hungry he was. He stopped talking and drank his orange juice. It tasted just like the kind they had in Vancouver. Then he looked at the cereal. There were two brand-new unopened boxes.

Ben's face lit up. Both of them had prizes inside. Mum usually bought the large economy boxes without prizes. Jimmy and he ate a lot of cereal. Mum said the prizes were junk and Ben knew she was right, but he liked them, anyway.

Taking his time, he studied the pictures on each package. One was a kind of dart thing. It said it would shoot from three to four metres. The other was a little plastic spaceman. Ben chose the one with the dart in it. He could choose the other one tomorrow, if Aunt Rose didn't mind. He opened the box and peered inside. He couldn't see the dart. It must be buried under the cereal.

"Go ahead and dig for it," his aunt told him. "I bought them especially for you. Your hands are clean, aren't they?"

Ben started to nod. Then he remembered that he had not washed before he came down. And his right hand was covered with dog germs. He blushed.

"Never mind." Aunt Rose took down the hand towel hanging by the sink, wet it and handed it to him. "I didn't show you where your towels were last night, so it's as much my fault as yours. Give them a lick and a promise with this."

As he took the towel and scrubbed his hands hard, Ben wondered whether Aunt Rose knew about Gully's visit to his room. Was that why she said a *lick* and a promise? He didn't think so. He decided not to say anything about it. If he did, she might think he had made friends with Gully. He hadn't.

When he fished out the dart, it was very small, much smaller than the one in the picture. It looked as though it might break the first time you used it. And you had to have an elastic band to make it go. Aunt Rose got him one. Ben shot it the way the directions said. It only went a little way and then nose-dived to the floor. But it did work. It was better than nothing, whatever Mum said.

He poured the cereal into his bowl. Then he looked for the white sugar. He couldn't see any. Dad had said it was rude to ask for things that were not on the table. Ben tried brown sugar. He liked it.

When he had finished, he dried the dishes while his aunt washed. Once they were done, he asked if he could watch TV.

"I'm afraid not," Aunt Rose said. "I don't have a television."

Ben stared at her. No TV? Was she kidding? Everybody had a TV.

Aunt Rose chuckled.

"I know," she said. "You can't imagine life without television. But when I decided to give up teaching, move back here, turn the upstairs into an apartment and try writing full time, I couldn't afford both a computer and a television. So no TV."

Well, at least she had a computer. That was something.

"You know, when I was your age, not everybody had a TV set. We didn't get one till I was eleven or twelve," Aunt Rose said.

Ben knew. Dad had told them, over and over, about not wasting his time on cartoons when he was a kid. Still, it was hard to picture.

"What did you do?" he said.

"Lots of things," his aunt said. "We put on plays. We built huts in the bush near our house. We went for hikes. We read a lot of books. Comic books, too. I found some of our old comics in a carton the other day and I put them in your room. They're in the big box beside the chest of drawers. But today is so lovely and sunny. It's a shame to stay inside. Why don't you go out in the backyard and play with Hana?"

"Who's Hana?"

"She lives next door," Aunt Rose said. "She's a couple of years older than you are, but she's the only child who lives at this end of the street. She's been asking and asking when you'd get here ever since I told her you were coming for a visit."

Ben did not want to play with some strange girl. He hated the way grown-ups tried to make you be friends with kids before you had a chance to find out what they were like. She sounded sappy, asking and asking when he'd get there. Yuck! Not only that, but if she was the only kid around, she must be the neighbour child who was playing with Gully. He definitely was not interested in playing with either girls or dogs. Besides, he had that trap door to think about. He did not meet his aunt's eyes.

"I think I'll go up and find those comics," he said. "I don't feel like playing outside right now."

As he headed for the stairs, though, he had to pass the kitchen window. He might as well take a quick look at this Hana. He paused and then came to a full stop.

The backyard was empty.

Where was Gully? The girl couldn't have taken him for a walk. With a small shiver Ben remembered how hard Gully had pulled on his leash the night before. No kid would be strong enough to hold onto him, if he decided to take off.

Then Ben saw the dog. He was in the yard after all. He came charging out from behind some bushes. He had a stick in his mouth. He ran in big leaping bounds. His caramel-coloured ears flew back. His tail waved joyously even while he was running. He held his head high in the air as if he wanted the whole world to see what a fine stick he had. Even Ben could see that he was having a wonderful time.

"Fetch, Gully. Bring it here," a voice called.

Then Ben saw the girl, too. She had been standing right up against the house, just to the right of the window. As she went to meet Gully, he got a good look at her.

She was bigger than he was. Her hair was long and straight and very black. It hung in bangs. She had on faded blue jeans. The T-shirt she wore had writing on it. As she stopped and turned sideways to him, Ben made out the words:

HANA UCHIDA

CHAMPION NUT

6

Hana Spills the Beans

*H*ana Uchida had a stick in her hand like the one Gully was fetching. She was waving it in the air and laughing.

Ben stayed at the window, watching. Gully raced up and slid to a stop right in front of Hana. He dropped his stick at her feet. Then he jumped up at her, trying to snatch the one she was still holding.

Ben shrank back. He expected to see her drop the stick and run for the house. She took a quick step backward instead.

"No, you don't, you big dope," Hana shouted at the excited dog. "Down! Down, I said!"

Ben's eyes stretched wide. He could not believe it when Gully backed up and went down on all his four feet. His pleading gaze went from the girl's face to the stick and back again. But he stayed down.

"Good boy!" Hana said, as though Gully had done something brilliant. "That's more like it. Okay. Fetch!"

The stick sailed all the way to the back fence. Gully tore after it. He moved so fast that he almost got there ahead of the stick. Hana laughed. Then she picked up the stick he had dropped at her feet and stood ready. Back came Gully, ears streaming out like banners.

Ben sucked in his breath. Would the dog leap up at her again? When Gully jumped, he went so high that his head was level with hers. He could knock her over as if she were a bowling pin. If he did knock her down, what would he do to her once she was on the ground?

Aunt Rose didn't seem worried. She was putting the clean dishes away, paying no attention to what was going on outside. Didn't she understand how dangerous dogs could be?

Gully did not knock Hana down. He dropped his stick neatly and just stood there, all his muscles bunched up, ready to chase the stick in her hand.

"Hana does love animals," Aunt Rose said from just behind Ben. She had come to watch the pair in the yard, after all. "She wants to be an animal trainer when she grows up. Most of the time, anyway. She does change her mind. It's a shame she can't have a pet of her own."

"Why can't she?" Ben asked, although he did not really care.

"Her parents think an animal would tie them down too much. They like to go skiing during the winter, and they travel quite a bit. Her father's family are still mostly in Japan, so they go there to visit every two or three years. Hana's very fond of her Japanese grandmother. But nothing makes up for not having a dog."

Hana had to be crazy, Ben thought.

Yet even though the game with the sticks did look frightening, it looked as though it might be sort of fun, too. Maybe he wouldn't mind throwing sticks for a dog if it was a very small dog and if he could be absolutely sure it would always drop the sticks nicely and never jump up or snap.

But you couldn't be absolutely sure of anything with dogs.

Now that dumb Gully was teasing Hana by bringing the stick to her, dropping it, and then grabbing it up before Hana could get it. Once he had it, he raced off in excited circles, looking back at the girl over his shoulder. Ben almost laughed. It was so plain that Gully wanted Hana to chase him and try to recapture the stick.

Aunt Rose did laugh.

"What a tease that dog is!" she murmured.

Hana pounced, doing her best to grab the stick. Gully held on and growled at her. Ben heard the growl right through the window. He stiffened. Aunt Rose put her hand on his shoulder.

"He's only playing," she told him. "Don't worry. Hana knows how to handle him."

Ben did not say anything. He had forgotten all about the box of comics upstairs. He had even forgotten about the mysterious trap door. He leaned closer to the window.

Hana got hold of one end of the stick and pulled hard. Gully growled again. His tail was still wagging, but Ben did not notice. The second growl was louder than the first. It sounded ferocious. Ben could not believe his eyes when Hana let go of the stick and smacked the big dog across the nose with her open hand. Wasn't she afraid of anything?

"Bad boy! Cut that out," she scolded. "We are not playing Tug-of-war. We are playing Fetch. *Drop it!*"

Gully looked sad. But he had gotten the message. If he wanted to go on playing any game with Hana, he'd have to let her have the stick. It landed on her left sneaker.

"Ouch," Hana said, but not as though it really hurt. Then she added, "Good boy, Gully!"

Gully gave a small prance. But his eyes never left the stick. Finally it went winging through the air again. He dashed after it.

"Wouldn't you like a dog like that, Ben?" Aunt Rose asked softly. "You see now how playful and gentle he is."

The very idea shocked Ben. Everybody knew how he felt about dogs. Even Aunt Rose should have it straight by now. He opened his mouth to tell her exactly how much he hated dogs when Hana turned and spotted him at the window. Her face split in a broad grin. She waved.

"Hi!" she called. "Come on out and play with us."

Ben stared back at her. He shook his head. If only he had gotten away before she saw him!

"What's the matter? Are you sick?" she shouted, coming closer.

Ben felt trapped. He shook his head again and did his best to look unfriendly. The moment she turned away, he'd beat it up the back stairs to find those comic books.

Hana bent down and spoke to the dog.

"That's enough for now, Gully," Ben heard her say. "I have to go inside for awhile."

She was coming in. What if she brought that dog in with her?

"No, Gully," he heard her say then. "Miss Tucker told me to leave you outside. But I'll come back soon, I promise."

Then she was in the kitchen. She looked shy all at once. Ben felt shy, too. He tried to think of a good reason for not going back out with her.

"Ben, this is my next-door neighbour, Hanako Uchida,

known around here as Hana," Aunt Rose said. "Hana, you are so good with Gully. Tell Ben how gentle he is. He won't believe me."

"Gully is the most wonderful dog I know," Hana said. "He is so smart. He understands every word I say. Don't you think he's fantastic, Ben?"

Ben looked away from her. He felt dumb. It was his business how he felt about dogs, not Aunt Rose's or this girl's.

"He's okay, I guess," he mumbled, glaring at a little cactus plant on the shelf by the sink. "I don't like dogs much."

Hana stared at him as though he had suddenly grown two heads.

"You don't like dogs?" she gasped. "How can you not like dogs? Dogs are my favourite animal. Anyway, you'll have to get to like Gully, won't you? He's going to be your birthday present. Boy, are you lucky!"

7

Thunderstorm

*B*en stared at Hana. What was she talking about? Gully was not his birthday present. His birthday was not until September. And, anyway, Gully was Bob's dog.

"You're crazy," he said at last. "Gully's not my dog. And it isn't my birthday."

But Hana was not looking at him. She was looking at Aunt Rose. And her face had turned crimson.

"Oh, Miss Tucker," she wailed, "I'm sorry. I didn't mean to tell. It just popped out. I forgot all about it being a secret."

Aunt Rose sighed and shook her head. She looked from Hana's worried face to Ben's puzzled one. She laughed suddenly. Then she pulled out a chair and sank down on it.

"It's all right, Hana," she said. "Poor Ben. He doesn't know what we're talking about. I'd better explain."

Ben waited. But she took a minute to get started.

"Gully is Bob's dog," she said. "But Bob and his wife have to move to England and they can't take Gully with them. They would have to leave the poor dog in quarantine for six months, and that wouldn't be fair to him. So Bob and his wife are looking for a new home for Gully. And I thought of you and Jimmy, especially you."

Ben stared at her. His mouth opened but no words came out. Aunt Rose went on quickly.

"Oh, I knew you weren't crazy about dogs. I called your father and asked him if I could give Gully to you for your birthday. He told me that they would like you to have a dog and that Jimmy has wanted one for ages. But he said that you were frightened of them. No dog, he said."

Now Hana was staring at Aunt Rose, too.

"You didn't tell me he said no," she whispered.

"Well, no, I guess I didn't," Aunt Rose admitted. "You see, I couldn't believe anyone could stay scared of Gully. I thought I'd invite him and Ben here together and, once they got to know each other, everything would be different."

Hana turned and looked straight at Ben, her brown eyes searching.

"Are you scared of dogs?" she demanded.

Ben looked down at his feet. He felt his cheeks grow hot.

"No, I'm not scared of dogs," he lied. "I just don't like them. I don't want one, that's for sure!"

"You really don't want a dog?" Hana said. "You don't want Gully?"

Ben raised his head and glared back at her. Why didn't she mind her own business? He could hate dogs if he felt like it.

"I hate dogs," he flung at her. "They're vicious. They can even kill people. I saw it in the paper, so there!"

Hana tossed her head.

"We're talking about Gully," she said. "Gully isn't vicious, for Pete's sake. Gully wouldn't hurt a fly. People sometimes kill people, too. Does that make you scared of me? I'm a person. Boy, are you dumb!"

"I am not!" Ben yelled. He was so mad that he was afraid he might cry. He wanted to punch her as hard as he could.

"Okay, okay, cool down, both of you," Aunt Rose told them. "Just because you and I are nuts about dogs, Hana, doesn't mean Ben has to be, too. As for you, Ben, take it easy. Hana would love to have a dog like Gully. So it's hard for her to understand how you can pass him up."

She paused for breath. Neither Hana nor Ben spoke. Aunt Rose got up.

"Why don't we all have some oatmeal cookies and milk?" she suggested.

The two children still said nothing, but Ben stopped wanting to kick Hana. Although he had just finished breakfast, he was surprised to find he was starving. Maybe being mad made you hungry.

Aunt Rose got out the milk. Hana silently went to a cupboard and fetched the cookie tin. Then, as they started munching, Ben's aunt walked to the window and looked out. It was only then that Ben noticed that the room had grown much darker.

"Goodness, just look at that sky!" his aunt said. "I think we're in for a storm. Only an hour ago it was a lovely day. Now there's a real gale blowing."

Ben and Hana looked out the window. Ben was shocked to see great, purplish clouds piling up over half the sky. The tree branches were whipping back and forth. He could hear the wind. Then there was a sudden rumble of thunder, followed by a faint flicker of lightning.

Ben stiffened, clenching his hands until his knuckles went white. The other two didn't notice.

"I'll let poor Gully in," Hana cried, running to the back door.

"Wait a second, Hana," Aunt Rose called after her. "Ben, if you don't want to face Gully, you'd better go up to your room and shut the door."

Ben headed for the back stairs without a word. As he ran, he heard Aunt Rose begin to bang down windows. Then he heard Hana yell. She sounded scared.

"Miss Tucker, Gully's not in the yard," she was shrieking. "The gate's open and he's gone! I shut it when I came over. I'm positive I did!"

"I'm sure you did. It's blown open before, once or twice, when a gust of wind has caught it," Aunt Rose said hurriedly. "I forgot all about that when I told you to leave him out there."

"Oh, poor Gully!" Hana moaned.

"He's probably having the time of his life," Ben's aunt said, but her voice was worried. "Still, we'd better find him before he gets too far. I hope the rain holds off. He'll maybe go home, but there's nobody there to let him in. You look up the street in the other direction, Hana, and I'll go toward Bob's."

The back door slammed behind them. Ben heard them calling, "Here, Gully. Here, Gully." Then a spatter of rain drowned out their cries. Thunder growled again. It was closer this time.

Ben forgot all about Gully. He tore up the stairs to his room. He threw himself down on the bunk and buried his face in his pillow.

He was scared of the dark. He was scared of dogs. But he was terrified of thunderstorms. Lightning struck people dead all the time. It hit houses and killed people who thought they were safe inside. His parents said storms were beautiful and even Jimmy thought they were neat, but Ben hated them.

Suddenly he wondered if his window was still open. He lifted his head and took a quick look. It was! He could not make himself go over and shut it. The lightning might get him while he stood there.

Rumble. Bam!

Louder thunder! The open window was far too close.

Crash! He couldn't bear it.

Ben rolled over the edge of the bunk and scrambled underneath. It was dark there, and it smelled dusty. He rested his head on his arms. He was breathing fast. But the lightning would never come after him there.

Then, as his thudding heart quieted a little, he heard something totally unexpected. He heard a low whimper. He was not alone in his hiding place.

Gully was under there, too.

The Boy Who Hated Dogs

When Ben discovered that Gully was under the bed, he gave such a jump that he cracked his head hard on its sharp edge. Gully was pressed into the corner at the head of the bunk, but Ben could still have stretched out his hand and touched him. Gully was so close that Ben could hear every whimpering breath he drew.

He'd have to get out of there before Gully realized he had company. Maybe he could make it to the closet. He started to wriggle forward.

Bam! Crash! Crrrackle-BOOM!

Ben backed up so fast that he whacked his head again.

The storm sounded as though it were right in the room with them. Thunder was still rattling the window when a blinding pink glare of lightning flashed across everything Ben could see. He gasped and covered his face with his arm. He couldn't make himself go out there, Gully or no Gully. Not with the window wide open.

Rumble-grumble-BAM!

Ben was shivering now and fighting not to cry. He did his best to keep still so that Gully wouldn't notice him. He could not figure out why Gully had hidden under the bed in the first place.

Then, all at once, he guessed. Wasn't Gully shivering even harder than he was? Hadn't he himself heard the big dog whimper? As the lightning flashed next time, he watched the dog. He was sure he saw Gully cover his eyes with one of his giant paws.

Gulliver Gallivant was as scared of thunderstorms as Ben Tucker.

He's too big to be afraid, Ben thought. Then he remembered Dad saying, "You're too big to be such a crybaby, Ben." Being big did not help a bit.

The thunder roared again. Gully moaned.

"It's okay, Gully," Ben found himself saying. He did his best to sound like Dad. "Lightning usually just jumps from cloud to cloud. It hardly ever strikes things down here. By the time we see it flash, it's already struck, really."

Gully stayed scrunched down. There wasn't room to do anything else. But when Ben spoke to him, his tail gave a feeble thunk against the floorboards. And, the next moment, he began to creep toward Ben. The boy hesitated, and then kept talking.

"You can even tell how far away the storm is. If you can count in between the lightning and the thunder, then it isn't too close. You have to count like this. One-thousand-and-one. One-thousand-and-two."

Ben was amazed. He sounded just like a grown-up. He went on, not really sure whether he was talking to Gully or himself. Although Gully was touching him now, he did not shift his position.

"This is only sheet lightning, too. At least, I think it is. My father says sheet lightning never hurt ..."

This time the flash of lightning came right on top of the crack of thunder. Without stopping to think, Ben clutched at Gully. His face went down onto Gully's warm fur and his arm wrapped itself around the dog's great neck. He did not remember that this was a dog and he was afraid of dogs. He just held on tight and waited for the lightning to strike them both.

Gully turned his head and gave Ben's ear a quick lick. Then they both waited.

The next peal of thunder was not quite so loud. Ben raised his head a little and listened. Could it be true? Was the worst part over already? It was. The storm, which had blown up so fast, was leaving as quickly as it had come.

Carefully, Ben loosened his grip on Gully's neck. Had he really been hugging a dog? He wriggled backwards a bit.

But Gully was still shaking. He did not understand that the storm was going away. His brown eyes met Ben's. Then the big Lab dropped his head onto his paws and gave a long sigh that ended in a little whimper.

"It's okay, Gully," Ben heard himself saying again. He stopped backing away. Gully's tail thunked once. Ben drew a deep breath. He reached out his hand and stroked the broad head.

"It's over, boy," he said. "It's all over."

Gully's tail whacked the floor twice, real wags now. Ben laughed. It was a shaky laugh but who cared? Nobody heard him but Gully. He tried scratching behind the velvety ear closest to him. Dogs were supposed to like that. Gully stopped trembling. He moved his head so that Ben's fingers would hit exactly the right spot. He grunted.

Ben laughed and scratched harder.

"Hey," he said softly, "you're not such a dragon, after all. You're a big marshmallow."

Then he heard a door downstairs bang shut.

"I couldn't find him," Ben heard his aunt say. "I'll call the animal shelter. He's only been gone for ten minutes, but maybe somebody has seen him."

"Hey, Miss Tucker, look! The front door's been open all along," Hana said. "Maybe he came into the house again!"

Ben did not wait for them to come up and catch him hiding under the bed. He slithered out, making as little noise as possible.

"Come on out, boy," he said softly over his shoulder. "They think you're lost. Do you want them to know you're a chicken?"

Gully stirred but stayed put. He could still hear the thunder, even if Ben couldn't.

Ben went to the door.

"Aunt Rose, I've found Gully," he called. "He's up here under my bed."

Had she heard him? Maybe he should go down. But he did not really want to leave Gully. Ben knew how much he hated being left alone when he was scared. If only he could coax the dog out from under the bed. If he sat down on the floor and talked to him, what would happen?

He might come leaping out. The thought of Gully back on all four feet made Ben stop to think. Gully quivering with fear was one thing. Gully wild and on the loose was quite another. Instead of getting down on the floor, he pulled a chair over to the bunk.

The next minute, Aunt Rose and Hana came running up the stairs. But when they reached the bedroom door, they stopped and just stood there, staring.

There sat Ben Tucker, the boy who hated dogs. On his feet rested the head of Gulliver Gallivant. And Ben was leaning down, scratching behind one of Gully's floppy ears.

9

Ben Takes Command

When Hana and Aunt Rose stopped in their tracks and stared, Ben could feel his face growing pink. He turned his head away from them. He gazed down at Gully, instead. Gully's tail banged the floor. The sound of it made Ben smile.

"Where did you find him, Ben?" Aunt Rose said then.

Ben wanted to hug her. She could have said, "How come you're sitting there patting Gully? Last night you wouldn't even stay in the same room with him." But she hadn't.

Hana did not give him time to answer. She was not tactful like Aunt Rose. She took a step forward and blurted,

"How come you're patting him like that? I thought you were scared of dogs. You said they were vicious!"

Ben scowled at her.

"I did not say I was scared of dogs. I said I didn't like them and I don't want one for a present. That's all I said."

He turned from her. He spoke to Aunt Rose.

"I think he must have gone out the gate and then heard thunder and run in through the front door," he said. "I found him hiding under the bed. He was away back in the corner, shivering and crying."

Hana dropped to her knees and flung her arms around Gully's neck. She rubbed her cheek on the top of his head. Her hair was wet with rain.

"Poor Gully," she crooned. "I wish I'd known. I'd have comforted you."

"That must have been what happened," Ben's aunt said. "I remember Bob saying that Gully's been afraid of storms ever since he was a puppy. It seems so silly in such a big dog."

Aunt Rose was just like Dad. If Gully were a boy, she'd say, "You're too big to be such a crybaby, Gully."

Gully had lifted his head off Ben's feet. He was busy licking Hana's face and right ear. He had wriggled forward and was now half out from under the bed. He did not look frightened any longer. Soon he'd be all the way out and back on his feet. Ben stood up and started to shift the chair.

Instantly the big dog scrambled out and gave a mighty

shake. Ben jumped away in spite of himself. Gully lying down, whimpering with fright, he could take. This Gully, so much taller, his mouth wide open so that his big teeth showed, all ready to romp and knock people over, he wanted no part of.

"You are so scared of him!" Hana cried, getting up, too. "I knew it. What a baby!"

Before Ben had a chance to answer back, she burst into giggles.

"Boy, it would have been a scream if you'd been scared of lightning, too, and hidden under the bed and then Gully had come running and crawled under there with you. I bet you'd have died on the spot!"

"Stop teasing him, Hana," Aunt Rose said. "It's a good thing he was here to comfort Gully since you and I weren't. I think that was very brave, Ben."

Hana stopped laughing and looked ashamed.

"That's right," she said, giving Gully another hug. "It's a good thing Ben wasn't scared. Right, boy?"

Gully looked at Ben. Ben looked at Gully. Ben had a feeling that even if Gully could have told on him, he wouldn't have. He smiled at the dog. He watched the long whip of a tail wag in response. If only the dog were not so big and rough, he might be okay.

"Hana," Aunt Rose asked, starting to leave the room, "can you stay for lunch?"

"No, I can't," Hana said. She looked worried all at once. "What time is it? I have to be home at ten to take my cousin to the library. It isn't past ten, is it?"

"You have exactly eleven minutes," Ben's aunt said. "Maybe Ben would like to go, too."

"No, he wouldn't," Hana said, before Ben had a chance to answer. "My cousin is four and he's a real pain. Mum has to stay home and babysit him all afternoon so I said I'd give her a break. It's a special story hour for pre-schoolers."

"I want to look at those comics," Ben said.

"I'll come over right after lunch," Hana told him. "See you then."

So who asked you? Ben wanted to say. But he kept quiet.

She ran off down the stairs. Aunt Rose paused and looked at the boy and the dog. Gully had not dashed off after Hana. He was standing looking at Ben and wagging his tail.

"I have to get us some lunch and make some sandwiches I've promised to send to the church this afternoon," Aunt Rose said. Then she went on in a soft voice. "Gully certainly seems to like you, Ben, even if you don't like him much. Shall I take him downstairs or may he stay with you?"

Ben opened his mouth to say she should take him. But before he got a word out, Gully lay down again by the chair and put his head back on his paws. Then he rolled his eyes up so he could look at Ben. His tail thumped the floor twice.

Ben did not want to be left alone with a dog. But Gully was trying so hard to be good.

"I ... I guess he can stay here," Ben said slowly.

Aunt Rose did not wait for him to change his mind. She left almost as swiftly as Hana had done. Ben and Gully were on their own.

Ben sat down quickly and didn't move for a full minute. Gully lay and watched him. He didn't look dangerous. But Ben did not trust him. He remembered the way the dog had leaped up at Hana, trying to snatch the stick from her hand.

At last he had to do something. He half turned in the chair, searching for the box of old comics. It was right beside the dresser, just out of reach. He would have to stand up and lean way forward to get his hand into it. Could he do that without disturbing the dog?

It took him a long minute to get up enough nerve. Then he stood up slowly and carefully.

At once Gully was on his feet. Ben froze. Gully waited for something to happen. Ben sat down again. Gully looked disappointed. But he sat down, too, still watching Ben.

Then Ben remembered Bob giving the dog orders. Hana had, too. The boy took a deep breath.

"Gully, lie down," he said.

He meant to speak firmly, but his voice squeaked and wobbled. Gully put his head on one side and seemed puzzled. Ben gulped and tried again. This time his voice came out in almost a shout. As he gave the command, he pointed at the floor, the way Bob had done the night before.

"Gully, *lie down!*"

To the boy's amazement, the big dog sank to the floor. He, Ben Tucker, had made this enormous dragon of a dog lie down. He could hardly believe it.

He looked at the dog stretched out at his feet.

"Stay, Gully," he said and stood up.

Gully looked mournful, but he did not get up. Ben didn't want to step over the dog to reach the comics. But he did manage to pull the box toward him until it was close enough for him to be able to reach in. There was a big pile of comics, a beat-up tennis ball and a dented mouth organ in the box. Ben quickly grabbed the top three comics and sat down.

He felt as if he had been running very fast.

Yet Gully, although he had watched Ben with interest, had not moved. It was wonderful.

Then Ben remembered the way Bob and Hana had praised the dog when he did what he was told. He leaned forward and ran his fingers lightly over Gully's broad head.

"Good boy," he said softly.

Whack, went the tail.

The comics were neat. Ben began to read about Captain Marvel. After a couple of pages he stole a look at the dog.

Gulliver Gallivant was sound asleep.

The Trap Door

Ben read two more comic books before he got bored. Gully was still asleep. Ben looked at his watch. It was ten minutes past eleven. He had lots of time to do something else before lunch.

The trap door! How could he have forgotten about it?

Ben studied the sleeping Lab. He looked so peaceful. Could he get away without disturbing him?

Keeping his eyes fixed on the dog, Ben eased himself up off the chair. Gully went on sleeping. He had rolled onto his side and was sprawled full length, snoring gently. He did not flicker an eyelash.

Ben took a deep breath and stepped over Gully's hind

legs. Gully snored on. Moving with great care, Ben crept forward one step at a time. Gully did not move.

Six seconds later Ben was out the door and crossing the hall to go up to the front of the house. He still moved on tiptoe. He was not sure Aunt Rose would like him exploring in her house without permission. But he didn't want to tell her. This was his private adventure. He wanted the trap door, and whatever lay above it, to be his secret.

He had to open the door to the apartment part of the house. As he reached for the doorknob, he listened hard. Aunt Rose chose that moment to turn on the radio down in the kitchen. Music poured up the stairs. Ben grinned. She'd never hear now. She might not stay in the kitchen, though. He'd still have to be careful. He turned the knob slowly until he heard the latch click open. The click sounded terribly loud.

He waited a moment, holding his breath. Neither Gully nor Aunt Rose came to investigate. He shut the door behind him but did not pull it tight. He didn't want any more loud clicks.

The wide hall stretched ahead of him. All he had to do now was walk to the front bedroom on the right. If only his steps didn't make the floorboards creak so much!

He was there. He closed the bedroom door behind him. Then at last he went into the closet and peered up at the small, square trap door in the ceiling, far above his head.

It was awfully high up, over twice his height. They sure built tall rooms in the olden days. If it weren't for the ladder, he would have no hope of reaching it. But there stood the ladder in the bedroom, ready and waiting.

It was a stepladder made of metal. It was much taller than he was. It was too heavy for him to carry, but he thought he might be able to push it across the floor. He tried shoving it a little. It shifted easily but it clanked and rattled. Well, the doors were shut. He'd have to take a chance.

Bit by bit, holding his breath and listening hard in case Aunt Rose called to ask what he was doing, Ben pushed the ladder across to the closet door. There he had to stop. The ladder, with its legs spread out, was too wide to go through the door.

Ben paused to think things over. If he turned the ladder and put it in step side first, it might work.

He had quite a struggle turning the ladder. Once it almost toppled over on top of him. Then, as the top of the ladder neared the door frame, Ben tensed. Was it going to slide under, or was it going to stick?

It just barely slid under. Perfect.

Ben checked to see that the ladder was placed right under the trap door. When he had it exactly the way he wanted it, he sat down on the bottom step for a moment to catch his breath. Sitting there, he tipped his head back and stared up at the distant opening. What would he really find up there?

Skeletons. That's what Jimmy would have told him.

But Ben wasn't scared. Not scared enough to give up, anyway. Besides, there wouldn't be anything too terrible in his own great-grandma's attic.

Then he remembered that other people had lived here after she died. Strangers had rented the house while Aunt Rose was living in Hearst. Maybe they had killed somebody and hidden the body up in this attic.

Ben forced a laugh. What a crazy idea. He'd never show Jimmy and Hana and Dad he wasn't a baby unless he got moving.

He stood up and squared his shoulders. He began to climb. When he got halfway up, he could feel his knees starting to shake. It looked so far down to the floor. But he did not stop. He just went more slowly. When he got to the second step from the top, he thought he could reach the ceiling. But first he'd have to let go of the ladder with both hands and straighten up to his full height. Could he?

It would help a lot if the ladder didn't keep trembling. Or did it only shake because he did?

He thought of Jimmy, of Hana saying, "What a baby!"

Very, very slowly, he straightened up to his full height. He felt dizzy. He had nothing to hold onto, only the flat wall. No, there were the shelves on his left, going almost all the way up. But if he reached over to them, he might lose his balance.

Biting his lips and bracing his knees against the very top of the ladder, Ben reached up his hands as high as they would go. His fingertips brushed something solid. He was touching the trap door!

He was so excited that he leaned back to look up, and wobbled wildly. He waved his arms for a moment, and then caught his balance again. He stayed very still and breathed slowly to steady himself. He counted to five. Then he reached up again.

He pushed at the wood with his fingertips. It didn't budge. He pushed harder with his whole hands. Suddenly, he felt it give a tiny bit. He was going to be able to open it. He shoved again, harder. He saw a crack open around the edge of the trap door and darkness beyond.

Then, below him, the bedroom door swung open. Gulliver Gallivant came padding into the room.

"Oh, no!" Ben gasped, staring down at the dog and swaying dangerously on the ladder.

Gully looked up and spotted him. His tail began to wag. He came over to the foot of the ladder and nosed around it.

At the same moment, Ben heard Aunt Rose.

"Benjamin Tucker," she called, "lunch is ready."

11

What to Do with Gully

Ben wanted to cry. Here he was at the top of a wobbly ladder. He had just gotten the trap door to move. And now Aunt Rose wanted him to come to lunch and Gully was at the foot of the ladder!

He couldn't climb down, not with that dog cutting off his way to the door. Soon Aunt Rose would come and find him. She would ask questions, and everything would be spoiled. His adventure was over before it had started.

But it wasn't. Not yet, anyway.

Gully had heard Aunt Rose calling, too. At the sound of her voice, his ears perked up. Then he spun around and went racing toward the kitchen.

The instant the dog was out of sight, Ben reached down and got hold of the top of the stepladder. Then he climbed shakily down. He ran after the dog, going lightly so that Aunt Rose would not know where he was coming from. When he got downstairs, he found his aunt spoiling Gully with a dog biscuit.

"Hi," she said, smiling at him. "Those old comic books must have been spellbinding. I haven't heard a peep out of you for hours."

Ben smiled back, but he did not look her straight in the eye.

"They were great. I've never seen such old ones before." He bit into his hamburger hungrily. Gully sat beside him and watched every bite going up to his mouth.

"You and Gully seem to have made friends," Aunt Rose said, handing him a bowl of salad.

"Mmmm. This is good!" Ben said, taking an especially large bite and chewing noisily. He didn't want to talk about himself and Gully.

Aunt Rose grinned at him and changed the subject. They talked about their favourite books. Ben loved *The Minerva Program*. Aunt Rose liked it, too. She said she couldn't choose just one favourite, though. She liked so many.

Then the phone rang. When Aunt Rose came back to the table, she looked worried.

"Ben, I'm afraid I have to go out this afternoon. Remember my telling you I had to make sandwiches? A member of our church died on Thursday and a group of us are providing refreshments for the family after the funeral. That call was from my friend Rhondda. Another woman who was supposed to help has sprained her ankle and Rhondda just found out. So they need somebody to take her place. I'm really sorry, because I wanted to spend the afternoon with you. But I can't let Rhondda down. She was going to pick up the sandwiches because my car is being repaired. So I told her she could pick me up, too."

Ben tried to make sense out of all this. Did it mean *he* was going to have to spend Saturday afternoon in church? Or would she let him stay home by himself? If she would, he'd be able to explore without worrying about getting caught.

But Aunt Rose hadn't finished.

"I know! I'll call Meg Uchida." Her look of worry disappeared. "Hana said she'd come over here, but instead you can spend the afternoon over there helping them to babysit her little cousin."

"I'd be okay here by myself," Ben said, trying not to sound too eager.

"I'm sure you would," his aunt said. "But I can't leave you here all alone."

"I'd have Gully," Ben said, to his own astonishment.

Aunt Rose laughed at him. She reached out and stroked Gully's soft ears.

"I'll let him out before I leave," she said. "When you go to the Uchidas', he can just stay here. Gully's used to spending time alone."

She stood up as if everything was settled, and got Ben a large bowl of strawberries and ice cream. Then she went to call Mrs. Uchida.

As Ben started on his dessert, he could hear her dial the number over and over.

"Meg is hopeless," she muttered, after trying the number for the sixth time. "I don't know what she finds to talk about. I'd better get into some decent clothes and try her again when I'm ready."

She vanished. Ben stirred his ice cream to make it soft. He loved it that way but Mum said it wasn't polite. Aunt Rose came back just as he finished the last spoonful. She let Gully out and then back in and returned to the phone.

Before she had time to dial, a car horn honked. Aunt Rose went to the front door, waved to her friend, ran back and snatched up a piece of paper. She scribbled a note on it and shoved it across the table at Ben.

"I can't get through to Meg and Rhondda's waiting," she said, grabbing up the tray of sandwiches. "The note explains everything. Take it next door as soon as you finish. Just pull the back door shut behind you. It'll lock itself. I know Meg won't mind having you. She'll be in all afternoon. I was talking to her this morning after Hana left. I'll be home around four o'clock, but if you're having fun, don't hurry back. I must fly!"

The next moment, the front door banged. She was gone. And he had the house all to himself.

Ben felt like singing. Mrs. Uchida didn't know he was supposed to be coming over so she'd never miss him. And he could get up to that trap door while Aunt Rose was out.

He made himself sit still and count to one hundred slowly just to be sure. Then he sprang up and ran to his room. Gully was at his heels, but he was too excited to care. He got his flashlight. Boy, would Mum ever have a fit if she knew how he was using it!

He went up to the room where the trap door was. Then he realized that he had to do something with Gully. What if the dog knocked over the ladder? Ben stared down at him, thinking hard. He didn't dare try to push him through the door leading out of the apartment. Gully might snap.

He went ahead of him instead, calling, "Come on, boy. You'll like it better out here."

Gully followed him eagerly. But the moment Ben turned to go back through the door, Gully wheeled about, too, and went ahead of him.

"No, Gully," Ben begged. "You stay out there."

He pointed. Gully looked to see what he was pointing at. Then he gazed up at Ben with puzzled eyes.

Ben had an inspiration. In the box of comic books, there was that old tennis ball. If he got the ball and threw it down the stairs, Gully would chase after it and he could shut the door on him before he got back.

He raced to his room and found the ball. The minute Gully spotted it, his eyes lit up and his tail wagged furiously. Ben felt uneasy. What if the dog leaped for it? He hurried back to the head of the stairs before Gully had a chance to think of trying any tricks and threw the ball all the way to the bottom.

It worked. Gully almost turned a somersault in his dash down after it.

But before Ben could get behind the door to the apartment, the dog had come flying back. He dropped the ball right at Ben's feet. He was so happy and excited that Ben had to pick it up and throw it a few more times.

It was a good idea, anyway. He would tire the dog out. Then Gully would fall asleep again and Ben would have his chance.

Away went the ball. Away went the dog, tumbling downstairs, galloping up again with it in his mouth. Soon the tennis ball was wet with spit. Ben picked it up gingerly. But Gully wouldn't let him give up quite yet.

The game grew so lively that Ben almost forgot the trap door. Then he noticed that Gully was getting out of breath. Good. Now if he could just get him to lie down ...

"Hi, Ben," called Hana's voice from the kitchen. "Hi, Gully. I'm back."

12.

Hana Is Scared

When he heard Hana call, Ben was so mad that he wanted to kick somebody. No, not just somebody. Hana Uchida. Who did she think she was, marching into his aunt's house as if she owned it? Who had asked her to come? Nobody. Who wanted her? Nobody. She'd wreck everything.

He'd have to get rid of her.

Maybe, if he just didn't answer, she'd give up and go away. He didn't think Hana was the kind of girl who gave up easily, but he stayed absolutely still and hoped.

Hana came into the downstairs hall. He watched her over the banister. She hadn't seen him.

Then Gully, impatient at the delay in their game, gave a small whimper of protest. Hana looked up. Ben did not smile. Her eyes widened in surprise. Maybe she'd gotten the message. But it wasn't Ben's scowl that had startled Hana.

"Hey, how come you're playing with Gully?" she demanded.

She was not pleased. Maybe she didn't want Gully to be friends with anybody but her. Ben wondered why the dog hadn't rushed down to greet her. Then he saw the reason. Gully's brown eyes had never left the ball. He was still waiting for the game to go on.

As if he played with dogs every day, Ben tossed the ball down the stairs. Gully flew after it.

"I guess I can play with him if I like," Ben said. "You were the one who said I was scared of him, not me."

Hana tossed her head. Her eyes flashed.

"If you weren't scared of him, why did Miss Tucker ask me to keep him outside so you, poor little sucky baby, could have your breakfast in peace. I guess Miss Tucker doesn't tell lies. Besides, your own father said ..."

Ben swung around and glared down at her. He could feel his face burning.

"You leave my dad out of this," he bellowed. "I never said Aunt Rose told lies. She made a mistake, that's all. Just because I didn't want a dog around when I was eating doesn't mean I'm scared of them. And I am not a sucky baby. I bet you wouldn't have nerve enough to do what I'm going to do in a minute, so there."

At once, Hana's dark eyes gleamed with interest. She came up the stairs almost as fast as Gully.

"What are you going to do? Tell me. I'll bet it's nothing much. Whatever it is won't scare me, that's for sure."

Ben was mad at himself now. Why had he gone and said such a dumb thing? There must be some way to get out of telling her. If she'd just give him time to think, he'd come up with something.

But she didn't give him time. Instead she burst out laughing as he hesitated.

"I knew it!" she crowed. "You can't think of one thing to say, can you? What a baby! Bragging about nothing."

"Follow me," Ben growled and led the way through the apartment door. She followed him without a word. So did Gully. Once they were inside the front bedroom, Ben grabbed her arm and jerked her forward to the foot of the ladder. Then he pointed up to the trap door, high above them.

"See that trap door? I'm climbing up to find out what's up there."

Hana's eyes widened. She pulled her arm free and backed up a step.

"You can't go up there. Miss Tucker won't let you."

Ben couldn't believe it. Hana sounded nervous.

"Aunt Rose has gone out," he said. "I'll be up and down again before she gets home. She won't be back till around four o'clock."

Hana bit her lip and looked at him sideways. Ben felt great.

"The ladder doesn't go high enough," she said.

She was scared. She really was. Who was the baby now? Not Ben Tucker.

"You can come, too," he said, keeping his face straight. Then, looking her in the eye, he added softly, "Or are you too chicken?"

She looked so terrified that he almost burst out laughing. He couldn't believe he had beaten her this easily. What was the matter with her?

Wait a minute. He didn't really want her to climb up there with him, did he?

Suddenly, he knew that he did. It would be more fun with two. He'd have to talk fast, though, to persuade her. She wasn't even pretending now not to be scared. Yet this was the girl who had whacked Gully across the nose when he wouldn't give her the stick.

"The ladder goes a long way up," he told her. "You can reach the edge of the trap door from there and get a grip on it with your hands. I already tried that before lunch so I know. You're bigger than I am. It should be even easier for you. Once we get that far, then we can go up the last bit by swinging our feet over and using the shelves. See?"

He pointed to the shelves that went up the side of the closet. Hana barely glanced at them.

"They don't look all that strong," she objected. She added more loudly, "They don't go all the way to the top, either."

"They do, too. Use your eyes," Ben told her. "And they're plenty strong enough. My great grandmother used them to put heavy things on for years and years. Would I trust them if they weren't safe? No way. Any other excuses?"

"It's awfully dark up there!"

He fished his flashlight out of his pocket and shone it up so she could see how bright it made things. But she still didn't look convinced.

"My mum would be mad," she said. "It doesn't look safe. I hate climbing up things. I'm not allowed to climb trees. My dad fell out of a tree when he was a kid and broke his arm in three places."

"So what?" Ben said. "This isn't a tree. Anyway, I knew all along that you wouldn't have the nerve. So go ahead and stay down here where you won't get hurt. I'm going up."

He dropped his flashlight back into his deepest pocket. He needed both hands free. He put one foot on the bottom rung of the ladder. Something bumped into it, making it jiggle. He glanced down.

It was Gully.

Ben took his foot off the ladder. What if Gully got all excited and jumped at the ladder and made it rock when he was at the top? Ben's stomach lurched at the very thought.

"Help me put Gully out of this part of the house," he said gruffly to Hana. "I don't know how to get him to leave."

"Boy, are you helpless!" she said, sounding like herself again. She took Gully by his collar. "Come on, Gulliver."

Gully trotted along happily. When they reached the door out of the apartment, Hana opened it and she and Gully walked through. She pointed at the floor and started to order Gully to lie down.

Then Ben saw her hesitate. Gully was gazing up at her as if his heart was breaking. Even Ben could tell that Gully did not want to be left out there all by himself. Hana looked up at Ben.

"I'll be back in a second," she said.

She ran down the stairs. Gully looked after her, went down a couple of steps, swerved and returned to Ben who was standing in the doorway. He was staring hard at Ben's pocket, the one bulged out by the tennis ball. Ben pretended not to understand.

What was Hana doing? Had she chickened out and gone home? He was surprised at how much he wanted her to come back.

Suddenly a blare of music made him jump. Then he heard a voice saying, "This is CJOY in Guelph, Ontario." Hana came running back, a wide smile on her face. When she reached the landing, she called Gully and made him lie down. Then she gave him a big cookie. While he crunched it, his tail thudding the carpet, she slipped through the door and closed it behind her.

"I put the radio on to keep him company," she said. "That's what my aunt does for her canary."

On the far side of the door, Gully whimpered.

"Be a good boy and stay, Gully," Hana called to him.

They both heard the dog give a great sigh. Then he flopped back down on the floor.

Ben had had enough of Gully. He spun around and marched back to the room that used to be his great-grandmother's. He was glad now that Hana was there. It *was* dark inside the closet. That morning the sun had been shining through the front window and it had been much brighter. But now the sun was on the other side of the house, and even the room outside the closet seemed shadowy.

Ben closed the bedroom door tightly this time. Then he went straight to the stepladder. Without giving himself a chance to think it over, he began to climb.

Hana stood at the bottom and stared up at him, her eyes wide. Somehow that made the climb easier.

He was at the top. He pushed the trap door. It moved. He managed to shift it a little. All he could see through the crack was darkness. He had his flashlight, though. Should he shine it through the crack before he tried swinging up?

"Oh, Ben," Hana quavered from the foot of the ladder, "I don't think you should go up there. What if Miss Tucker finds out? Or my mum? We'll be in big trouble."

Ben knew then that if he waited to get out his flashlight, he'd lose his nerve. He held onto the crack with both hands, swung his feet onto the first shelf, then the second. Then he freed one hand and gave the trap door the hardest shove he could. It banged up, showering his face with bits of dirt. And with a great scramble with his feet and hoist with his hands, Ben was through the trap door.

He sat on the edge, his heart pounding so hard he felt it might burst. Then he looked down between his knees at Hana's anxious face far beneath him.

"So who's a sucky baby now?" he said.

13

Trapped

Ben laughed down at Hana, but really he was scared. What would he see when he flashed the light around up here? It sure smelled queer and dusty.

"What's it like?" Hana was asking. "What do you see?"

He got out the light. His hands were not steady so he gripped it tightly. Suppose he dropped it? The very thought made him feel cold all over.

Click.

A streak of light sprang across the darkness, making Ben jump. He swung the light in a wide arc so that it swept the whole space. It was like a big empty cave up there. He was sitting on a beam that went right across the attic. The roof sloped down to the floor away out at the edges and met at a ridge pole far above him. Other beams crisscrossed the floor and in between them was a lot of brown matted stuff.

Ben stretched out his hand and touched some of it. It was rough. It had prickly bits in it. He pulled his fingers back and rubbed them on his jeans. Insulation! That was what it was. They'd put some in their house in Vancouver to help keep the fuel bills down. He had felt it then and it had made his hand sting just like this.

He flashed the light into the far corners. No skeletons. No treasures, either. But it was a neat place. As his eyes got used to the darkness, he saw that there were gaps here and there around the edges. He could see bits of daylight through them. There was nothing to be scared of up here. And he had discovered this great place by himself.

Suddenly he remembered Hana. He peered down at her.

"Come on up," he urged. "It wasn't hard, honest. You won't fall. It's neat up here. Come on. Just try."

He could tell she was wavering. He kept talking.

"You can see for yourself that it's safe. If I can do it, you can. You're taller. It's really neat up here. You've got to see it."

"Is it ... what's up there?" she asked.

Ben hardened his heart. The only way to get her up was to keep her curious. And to make her ashamed, too, of not being as brave as he was. It would be lots more fun with two of them. If she stayed down there, he'd have to go down, too, and the adventure would be over.

"Hurry up," he snapped at her. "You'll like it. I can't explain it. You have to see it for yourself. Don't be such a big suck."

She glowered at him. Good. If she got mad enough, she'd do it just to show him. He waited.

"I can help you with the last bit," he put in. "You can grab my hands and I'll haul you up."

Hana clutched each side of the ladder and started up. Her jaw was set. She was staring straight ahead and breathing hard. Then, as she got to the top, she glanced down. Ben heard her gasp. Then she seemed to freeze.

He couldn't think what to do. He could see the ladder beginning to shake. If he didn't figure out some way to help, she might lose her grip and fall.

He swung himself over on his stomach and reached down both hands.

"Grab hold," he yelled at her. "Come on!"

Hana snapped out of her trance. She ignored his outstretched hands. She gulped in a sobbing breath, grabbed the edge of the opening and began to swing up the way he had done.

Crack!

The shelf creaked under her weight and began to give. Hana screamed and sprang up to the top one. It came loose and crashed down on the one beneath. Before it went, she was up through the opening, half in, half out. Ben pulled at her with all his strength and she gave one final desperate wriggle. She was safe!

Ben was so terrified that he couldn't speak or move. Hana began to cry in noisy sobs.

"I knew we shouldn't," she wailed. "I told you it was dangerous. My mum will kill me when she finds out!"

Ben sat up. Where had the flashlight gone? He couldn't have let it fall, could he? No. It was right beside him. He picked it up and turned it on. He pointed the beam at Hana.

"Stop crying," he said. Then he heard himself add, "You're too big to be such a crybaby."

That made him laugh. It wasn't much of a laugh but he knew that it was better than crying.

"I'll go down," he told Hana, "and get help."

Hana clutched at him.

"No!" she shrieked. "Don't leave me alone up here. Besides, you'll fall and get killed."

Ben looked down at the shelves. The top one had landed on the second one, the one that had made that awful cracking sound. Hana must weigh a lot more than he did. They had felt perfectly safe to him. If he hung by his hands, his feet would reach the ladder. But suppose he couldn't find it? He was no good at gym. He knew he couldn't pull himself back up to safety if the ladder wasn't right there. It was a very long way to the floor.

"Okay," he said. "I'm not going anywhere. For Pete's sake, pipe down. There's nothing to worry about. Aunt Rose will be home soon. She'll get us down."

Hana's sobs grew a little quieter. Soon they were more like sniffles.

"I thought you said she wouldn't be home till after four o'clock," she muttered. "I came over about two. That means we'll be trapped up here for hours!"

Ben sat still. He thought of something he had heard Dad say often.

Stop panicking and try thinking.

"We don't have to just sit here," he said. "Maybe we can call out to somebody through those cracks where the light's coming in. But I think we'd better crawl along the beams. I don't know what's under the insulation. It might not be safe."

Hana eyed the insulation and refused to move.

"We might crash right through the ceiling and be killed," she said.

Ben gave her a look of disgust. Then he went ahead on his hands and knees. The beam was wide and perfectly safe. He made it to one of the gaps.

But when he tried to see through it, all he glimpsed was another bit of roof. Some light shone through the narrow crack, but he couldn't get his hand through it or see anything clearly.

"Help!" he called through the crack. "Help!"

His voice screeched up high like a baby's. He felt really dumb. Hana giggled. Still, it sounded better than her bawling, he told himself. He kept his back to her.

They both hushed and sat still, listening. Far, far away, Ben thought he heard a car horn. That was all.

"Try again," Hana told him.

"You try," he growled and backed up to let her by. But nobody heard Hana, either.

They got to three of the small gaps. Their shouts soon grew weak. Finally they crawled back to the trap door and sat there, staring at each other in the dim light.

Ben looked at his watch with the flashlight. It was hard to see. It was only five minutes past three.

"I knew I never should have come up here," Hana sniffed, on the verge of tears again.

Ben didn't answer. He was looking at his flashlight. Now he knew why he had had trouble seeing the time. The light was much dimmer. He was wearing out the batteries. He clicked the light off. The darkness seemed to press in around them.

"Turn it on," Hana cried. "It's too spooky up here in the dark."

Ben switched it back on. What would he say when Hana noticed that the beam of light was much weaker? He had no idea.

14

A Call for Help

They were trapped in the attic and Aunt Rose would not be home for nearly an hour. Ben's heart sank. Any second now, dumb old Hana was going to start bawling again.

He wanted to shake her. Why couldn't she make the best of things? If she'd just try …

That was what Dad had asked him to do. Had Dad wanted to shake him? Probably. He remembered his father's face looking at him yesterday. Ben swallowed hard.

Then he had an idea.

"Knock, knock," he said.

"What?"

"I said 'Knock, knock,' dummy. You're supposed to say ..."

"I *know* what to say. Dummy yourself," Hana snapped. Then she added grumpily, "Who's there?"

"Ben."

"That's not a Knock, knock joke," Hana objected.

"Who says it isn't?" Ben asked. "Go on. Say 'Ben who?'"

"Ben who?"

"Ben to any good shows lately?"

Hana laughed. "That's not bad."

Ben grinned. He didn't tell her that Jimmy had made it up.

"You do one," he said instead.

They went through all the jokes and riddles they knew. Halfway through, when Hana was sounding happier, Ben explained about the batteries and turned the light off. Hana didn't like it. Neither did Ben, but he pretended he didn't mind. When they ran out of jokes, he switched it back on long enough to check the time. It was only twenty-two minutes past three.

For once, Hana came up with an idea.

"We could sing," she said.

Ben was not great at singing. Jimmy said he was always flat. But it was better than just sitting in the dark, waiting.

"You start," he told her.

She sang on and on. She knew all the hit songs. It turned out that she wanted to be a famous singer, as well as an animal trainer. Ben got tired of listening to her, but it was a lot better than hearing her cry. At least, he thought it was. After the sixth song, he wasn't so sure. He had a feeling Hana sang flat, too.

Finally four o'clock came. They leaned over the trap door opening, straining their ears. There was no noise from the house except a sound of distant music. Did that mean Aunt Rose had come home? Then Hana remembered turning the radio on for Gully. That was all it was.

The minutes crawled by. Hana had no more heart for singing. Ben could not think of a single riddle or joke. He was sick and tired of being up in that attic. He was thirsty and he needed to go to the bathroom.

At last they both heard a car door slam. It was a small, faraway sound, but they heard it. Ben went along the beam as fast as he could, in the direction of the sound.

"Aunt Rose, help!" he yelled. "We're trapped in the attic."

There was no answer. Ben scurried back to the trap door. They both listened. The noise from the radio got a bit louder. Had Aunt Rose turned up the volume? Hadn't she even noticed they were missing?

"Let's scream 'Help!' together. I'll count to three," Ben said. "One, two, three. *HELLLP!*"

They waited, holding their breath. Then Ben gave a groan.

"She thinks I'm over at your house. She told me to go there when I'd finished eating. She gave me a note for your mother. I stayed home because I wanted to come up here."

His voice trailed away miserably. Even though Hana was only a shadow in the darkness, he couldn't look at her.

"You mean she won't even miss you?" Hana demanded, her voice shrill.

There was a long silence. Then Ben heard Hana's breath catch in a sob.

"We'll be up here forever!" she whimpered.

Suddenly Ben remembered the note Aunt Rose had written for him to take to Mrs. Uchida. Where was it? Maybe he had left it on the kitchen table. She'd be sure to find it and guess something was wrong.

He opened his mouth to tell Hana. Then he changed his mind. Before he got her hopes up, he'd better check. He slid his hand into his right pocket. It was empty. Nothing in the left one, either. He found the scrunched-up piece of paper in his hip pocket. He left it there. He was glad he hadn't said anything.

"If only we hadn't shut both doors. If only I hadn't turned on the radio! Oh, Ben, maybe she'll never find us. I want to go home!"

"Who doesn't?" Ben muttered.

But another idea was coming to him. Hadn't he heard that dogs could hear better than people? He was sure he had. Somebody on TV had said that a dog's ears were seven times as sensitive as a person's. Maybe ...

He swung over so he was lying on his stomach. He stuck his head down through the hole in the closet ceiling as far as it would go.

"Gully, come!" he called. "Gully, *come*! Gulliver Gallivant, we need you! *Come!*"

Hana stared at him. Then she caught on and joined him. They kept shouting and shouting. Then Ben put his hand on her arm.

"Let's listen," he said.

They listened with all four ears. And then, at long last, they heard a door opening. Next, before they could scream again, they both heard paws leaping at the closed bedroom door below them. And they heard Aunt Rose say, "Gully, don't be silly. There's nothing in there."

Ben couldn't understand why Hana had to start crying again at that point. They were safe. They didn't even have to shout again. The moment Aunt Rose opened the door, she saw the ladder. The next minute she was gazing up at them.

"What on earth ..." she began.

Then Ben understood Hana better. Tears stung his eyes, too, at the sight of his aunt. He cleared his throat.

"We came up here exploring," he told her in a husky voice, "and we can't get down."

Aunt Rose climbed up the ladder and held onto them as first Hana and then Ben lowered themselves through the opening. The ladder did wobble a bit, but Aunt Rose didn't seem worried. She felt so strong and steady that Ben flung his arms around her neck and gave her a great hug.

Aunt Rose hugged him back with her free arm.

"Goose!" she said. "I never expected to find you up there. Gully kept running to the stairs and whining. Then he led me straight to the door. I wonder how he knew."

Ben smiled down at the dog.

"I called, 'Gully, come,'" he said. "And he did what he was told."

15

A Different Dragon

Gully was waiting at the foot of the ladder. He wagged his tail like mad when he saw Hana. But when Ben reached the ground, the dog seemed to go crazy with joy. He leaped up and licked Ben's chin. Ben shrank back against Aunt Rose and watched in horrified fascination as Gully shot off around the room in dizzy circles. Ben was sure he would crash into the wall at any moment, but Gully went whizzing around, just missing everything.

"What's wrong with him?" Ben demanded shakily.

Aunt Rose laughed.

"He's so pleased with himself that he can't stay still," she said. "Gully, you idiot, calm down."

She moved toward the speeding dog. Ben sprang after her for protection. Gully, swerving around her, found Ben directly in his path. The dog tried to stop in time but couldn't. He whammed one shoulder into the boy. Then Ben was flat on the floor with Gully peering down at him.

For one paralyzed second, Ben stared up at the dog looming over him. Gully's wide open mouth seemed enormous and full of jagged fangs. His great ribbon of a tongue practically touched Ben's nose. He felt Gully's hot breath fanning his face. All his terror of the huge dog came flooding back. He shut his eyes and waited for the dog to pounce.

"Come here, Gully, you big goof," Ben heard Hana say.

"This is between Ben and Gully," Aunt Rose said quietly. "You come with me, Hana. Your mother must be wondering where you are."

Ben, afraid to move or even breathe, could not believe they were deserting him. But then he heard their footsteps leave the room, Aunt Rose's swift, Hana's dragging a little.

He couldn't keep holding his breath any longer or he'd burst. He let it out gradually and waited. Nothing happened. Ben opened his eyes a crack. He was peering straight up into Gully's face. And Gully didn't look dangerous. He looked worried. Ben blinked and opened his eyes all the way.

The dog pawed Ben's arm then. It didn't hurt. It was like a nudge, commanding him to sit up.

Ben lay still for one more long moment. Gully's paw poked at him again. Gully also blew on him, a long whistling breath through his nose. It reminded Ben of a horse. Moving very cautiously, he rolled over and propped himself up on one elbow. Now he and Gully were almost eye to eye.

Whack, whack!

That was Gully's tail hitting the door frame. Then the dog sat down and reached out his paw. He poked at Ben's arm. He wanted to shake hands. He wanted to say he was sorry. It had all been a big mistake. Was that really what he wanted? It looked like it. Gully gave him another, harder poke.

"Okay, boy," Ben said. Then he took the big paw and shook it solemnly.

At once Gully jumped up, tail waving happily, paws frisking.

Moving carefully, Ben got to his feet. As he started for the door, the dog romping around him, he knew he would never be so afraid of Gully again. He still wasn't sure about dogs in general, but this big, silly dog liked him too much ever to want to hurt him.

When they reached the kitchen, they found that Hana had not gone yet.

"I was so scared up in that attic," she was saying to Aunt Rose. "It sounds dumb, but I thought we might be stuck up there all night. Ben wasn't half as scared as I was."

Aunt Rose grinned at Ben.

"He's like me," she said. "I didn't tell you before, Ben, but your father and I went up there once. We did manage to get down by ourselves, but it was only thanks to me that we did. Your dad kept crying and saying we couldn't. I remember that I really was scared myself, but I never let him know. One person in a panic was enough."

Ben stared at her, wide-eyed. Dad in a panic! He could hardly believe it.

"Did you get in trouble?" Hana asked.

"We sure did, and that was John's fault, too. He knocked down some of Grandma's things. She came home and caught us trying to put them back. I still remember the look she gave us. It was a humdinger."

Ben knew that look. Was that where Dad had learned it, from his grandmother?

Hana went home then. Ben helped get supper. Aunt Rose handed him Gully's dish and told him how much dog food to measure into it. When Ben leaned down with the dish, the dog's big head plunged in before he could set it down. In two seconds every last morsel had vanished.

Even though the Lab had just finished his supper, he wanted some of theirs. He kept putting up his nose and sniffing hungrily at the stove, right next to Aunt Rose. She dodged him for a few minutes. Then she turned to Ben again.

"See if you can make him lie down over there in the corner. I'm afraid I'll step on him or spill something hot over him."

She said it so matter-of-factly that Ben did not protest. He had already moved this dog from one spot to another, after all. And he had watched Hana. He took Gully's collar in his hand and tugged gently.

"Come on over here, boy," he said.

Gully came as meekly as a lamb. And when Ben said, "Down, Gully!" he flopped to the floor with a grunt.

All evening Gully trailed Aunt Rose and Ben around. But it was Ben's chair he lay down beside at supper.

When the three of them went for a walk, Aunt Rose held the leash. When she told Gully to heel, he walked beside her more or less calmly. It looked so easy that Ben was about to ask if he could take the leash for the last half block. Then the dog, seeing home ahead, speeded up and tugged Aunt Rose along until she had to use both hands to slow him down. Ben was glad he hadn't spoken.

Once they went back inside, though, and Aunt Rose was reading out loud in the living room, it was Ben's foot that Gully used for a pillow. Ben didn't say anything but he couldn't help noticing. He was pretty sure Aunt Rose noticed, too.

That was why the boy was not surprised when Gully followed him to the foot of the stairs at bedtime. Ben paused. He waited to see if Aunt Rose was going to call Gully back to her.

"Good night, boys," Aunt Rose said.

When Ben got into bed, Gully settled down on the mat next to the bunk. Ben lay on his side so he could watch the dog. Gully slept curled up in a ball, nose to tail. Ben thought about his family coming the next day. Boy, were they in for a shock!

16

Ben Decides

When Ben came down to breakfast on Sunday, Aunt Rose didn't say good morning. She burst into song instead.

"Just a few more hours before your folks arrive,
A few more hours, as sure as you're alive!"

Ben grinned at her. She was pretty smart, reading his mind like that.

"Why don't we have pancakes to celebrate?" she said next.

Ben's grin got even wider. He loved pancakes next best to spaghetti.

"Hey, we never ate that cream I whipped to butter," he remembered.

"It will taste perfect on pancakes, don't you think," his aunt said, "with lots of syrup on top?"

It tasted fine.

After they had finished, Ben took Gully out in the yard. He wanted to see if he could get the dog to fetch for him the way he had for Hana. But before they could begin, Hana herself came running over.

"Come back inside. I've got something to tell you and Miss Tucker."

"But I'm just going to play with Gully," Ben protested. He looked at her sideways hoping he had surprised her.

"You can play later," Hana said in her bossiest voice. "Come inside now. This is important."

She ran toward the house, taking it for granted that he would follow. He had an urge to stay right where he was, but he was too curious. He followed her in. Gully came, too.

"Miss Tucker, guess what!" Hana began.

"You tell me. It's too early in the morning for guesses," Ben's aunt said.

"I'm going to be able to have Gully for my dog," Hana announced.

Ben felt shock jolt through him. Aunt Rose looked startled.

"Are you sure, Hana?" she said finally. "I was talking to your mother last night and she didn't say a word about changing her mind."

Hana reddened a little.

"Well, they did say I can have a dog," she said. "They still think Gully's too big. They want to get me a toy poodle. My mother doesn't want a dog that will shed hair on the furniture and my father says big dogs need too much exercise. But I just know I can make them change their minds, now that they've given in about letting me have a dog. I'll promise to brush him every day and walk him for hours and hours. When they know he has no place else to go, I'm sure they'll say it's okay."

The words ended abruptly as Hana ran out of breath and had to gasp for air. Aunt Rose couldn't help laughing. Hana looked hurt. And Ben, for some unknown reason, felt his heart start to sing.

"Hana, my sweet, a Labrador retriever is a far cry from a toy poodle," Ben's aunt said. "I'm sorry, but I don't think even you can talk your parents around that much. Labs shed hair in great gobs, even if you do brush them. And they do need more exercise than one eleven-year-old can possibly manage on her own. Besides, I'm pretty sure your mother is nervous around large dogs."

"Ben was scared of Gully, but he's changed," Hana argued.

Ben opened his mouth to protest, but stopped himself.

"Ben is one thing, your mother quite another. You know, Hana, poodles make wonderful pets. I know one that is just as good at retrieving as Gully. This dog chases after little balls and squeaky toys and brings them back over and over. It is every bit as big a pest as Gully."

Ben, watching Hana's face, thought he saw it brighten for one moment. Then the brief flicker of excitement died. She looked at Gully and sighed.

"I still think …"

"Don't. Give it up. Start getting pleased about a little dog instead. Gully just isn't meant for your family," Aunt Rose said firmly.

Hana looked stubborn.

"I don't see why you think Ben should have him then," she blurted, sticking out her bottom lip and glowering at Ben. "He hates dogs even more than my parents do."

Aunt Rose began putting away the clean breakfast dishes. She did not look at Ben.

"I think you already know why, Hana," she said over her shoulder. "For one thing, I know Gully belonged to a boy about Ben's age when he was a little puppy. I think he remembers. He certainly was drawn to Ben from the first. You must have noticed. Also, Ben's parents like large dogs. And his brother Jimmy has wanted a dog for years. He'll be pretty busy now with high school, but I know he'd love having a dog around. And Gully needs a family like Ben's. Those are my reasons. Now get along out of here, all of you, or I won't be ready for church on time."

When the three of them were outside again, Ben didn't know what to say to Hana. She looked grumpy. It wasn't his fault her parents wouldn't let her have Gully. So why was she mad at him?

"I've got to go," she muttered and took off.

He thought she wasn't even going to look back. Then she paused halfway up the back steps of her house, whirled around and shouted at him, "Good-bye. If you don't take him, you are out of your mind, Benjamin Tucker."

The door slammed shut behind her.

Gully did not let Ben stand staring after her for long. He fetched a large stick and thrust the spiky tip of it against Ben's limp hand. Ben got the message. He reached for it but, just in time, remembered to make Gully drop it first. Then he sent it skimming through the air. Gully fetched the stick over and over.

Once he did jump at it while Ben still had it in his hand. One of his teeth grazed Ben's thumb. Ben yelped and sucked his hand. Then he examined it for blood. The skin wasn't broken. All the same, he glared at the dog. He wasn't scared. He was just mad. Gully knew it. He sat down before Ben had a chance to scold him and held out his paw. Ben tried to look stern.

"You watch it, Gulliver," he growled. He shook Gully's paw up and down but forced himself not to smile while he did it. The big dope had to learn.

When Aunt Rose called them to come in, Ben felt as though they'd only been playing a few minutes. He glanced at the kitchen clock. He had actually been playing with a *dog* for three-quarters of an hour! A big dog, too.

They had to leave Gully behind while they went to church. Usually Ben found it hard to sit still during the boring bits in the service. But this time he hardly noticed them. He was too busy thinking. He tried imagining his family with a dog.

When there are storms, he thought, I could comfort him.

Gully met them at the front door. He jumped and danced around Ben, his tail wagging so hard it was a blur.

"It's a good thing I don't get my feelings hurt easily," Ben's aunt said. "That dog doesn't know I'm alive."

Ben was trying to fend off the excited Gully.

"Sit!" he bellowed.

Gully promptly sat, but he looked as though *his* feelings were hurt. Ben had to laugh.

He and Aunt Rose had lunch. Then he went up and read some more of the old comic books. Gully, looking bored, kept him company. Every so often Ben looked at his watch. Two-thirty. Three-twenty. At last it was getting near the close of the afternoon. He got up and went to the landing at the head of the stairs.

Plop!

Something dropped at his feet. The old tennis ball. He gazed down at the dog's brown eyes.

"All right, you pest," Ben said.

He tossed the ball to the foot of the stairs. Away flew Gully after it. The two of them were so busy playing that they didn't even hear the front door open.

"Well, Ben," said Dad's voice, "I see you've slain a dragon after all."

Ben looked down at them, his family. Mum was beaming up at him. She had missed him, too. Jimmy was staring, his face blank with shock. But his father's eyes, warm with approval, were on Gully. Playing it cool, Ben bent down, picked up the ball and threw it again.

"He's not a dragon. He's my birthday present," Ben Tucker said.